# GHOST HORSES

# GHOST HORSES

## PAMELA SMITH HILL

AN AVON CAMELOT BOOK

AVON BOOKS, INC.
1350 Avenue of the Americas
New York, New York 10019

First Avon Camelot Printing: April 1999

CAMELOT TRADEMARK REG. U.S. PAT. OFF. AND IN OTHER COUNTRIES, MARCA REGISTRADA,
HECHO EN U.S.A.

Printed in the U.S.A.

OPM 10 9 8 7 6 5 4 3 2 1

*For Emily, who gave me a title,*
*and for*
*Dorothy Selz and Holly Gentry*

# GHOST
# HORSES

# *Chapter 1*

Ernie Jones's Golden Girls performed at the Annual Corn Palace Exposition the night before, but I didn't get to see them. Papa brought us back to Uncle Henry's early, right after John Philip Sousa and before Mitchell's Loveliest Ladies danced the Maypole in Costumes of Enchantment.

"Heathen rituals," Papa had declared, dragging Mama and me away through more people than I'd ever seen in one place. He didn't mind that Cousin Artie and my brother Stephen stayed behind. But I wasn't surprised. Papa often said that young men needed to see something of the world before they made peace with the Lord.

"Tabitha, did you know that every one of those Golden Girls' costumes cost four hundred dollars?" Aunt Eleanor said the next morning, winking at me across the breakfast table. "Nothing to them but pearls. Says so right there in the *Daily Republican*."

I reached for the paper.

"It's an abomination," Papa boomed, and one long

arm flashed across the table, snatching the paper right out of my hands. "Ten years ago, no self-respecting newspaper in these United States would stoop to publish such trash." His voice rose. " 'There is no fear of God before their ways,' " he quoted, and his fist crashed down on the table. "I tell you, we live in a degenerate age, the end of the century when the coming of the Lord is at hand."

"I hardly think Mitchell, South Dakota, ranks with Sodom and Gomorrah, Brother Charles," said Aunt Eleanor, trying to suppress a smile. Aunt Eleanor and Uncle Henry thought Papa's religious beliefs bordered on the unintelligent. They, of course, were Unitarians. So was Mama, before she married.

"We live in a degenerate age, Sister Eleanor," he repeated, waving the newspaper dramatically, like he sometimes did on Sunday mornings when he shook his Bible high like a thunderbolt and told the congregation that every last man, woman, and child was a hopeless sinner before God Almighty. Papa was always more righteous during our visits to Uncle Henry and Aunt Eleanor's; he never stopped preaching.

"Please, Charles," Mama whispered, "you'll wake Eleanor's neighbors."

A section of the newspaper slipped out of Papa's grasp and floated to my feet. "Terrible Lizards: Heathen Hoax or New World Mystery?" the headline read.

I reached for the paper and carefully folded the headline out of sight. My heart began to pound. *Ter-*

*rible lizards. Those creatures Uncle Henry told me about last summer.* I had to read that article before Papa took it away from me.

"Excuse me, Aunt Eleanor." I edged toward the swinging door. "I'm not hungry. Excuse me, Mama, Papa?"

"Tabitha, you've barely touched your—"

But I was already out the door, taking the back stairs two at a time up to Artie's room where I'd be safe, where we could talk about it without interference from Papa. *Dinosaurs*, that's what Uncle Henry called them. Had they actually lived on the earth before Adam and Eve? Still, if Mr. Darwin was right . . .

I threw open Artie's door. "Look at this, Artie!" I gasped, unfolding the paper and sticking the headline under his nose. "Look what's in today's paper!"

Artie sighed and shook his head. "So?"

"Don't you see this headline? *'Terrible Lizards!'* " I perched on the edge of his bed.

"Sure, everybody knows about them. Dad got a whole book on them sent out from New York after Easter. Pictures and everything."

"Why didn't you tell me?"

Artie laughed. "Didn't know you were interested."

"But last summer, when we were looking for fossils . . . Don't you remember?" Artie had always been my friend, my confidant. The one person who understood how much I wanted to study science, to be a professor like Uncle Henry. Why didn't he remember? Was it because of that new girl—Janette—with her perfect golden ringlets and a whole wardrobe of frocks with puffed sleeves?

"Come on, you goose," Artie said. "Let's go down to Dad's study." He pulled me to my feet. "But I don't know *why* a girl like you wants to know about monsters. You ought to be thinking about getting yourself a beau."

Yes. It had to be Janette. Artie seemed different from the first moment he met us at the station. He seemed a lot more interested in socializing than talking about our plans to study science together back East. I followed him through the long, dark hall and together we tiptoed down the front stairs. I heard Papa's voice rising and falling all the way from the kitchen; Uncle Henry must have gotten up extra early and slipped away to avoid another one of Papa's impromptu breakfast sermons.

Artie opened the study door soundlessly and we glided inside.

I had always loved this room. Dark. Mysterious. Lined with books and smelling pleasantly of Uncle Henry's pipe. We had nothing like this back home in Rim. For the most part, Papa distrusted books and too much learning. "Everything you need to know," he said, "is right here in the Bible."

But Uncle Henry had understood, and he'd lent me books. Lots of them. That's how I got to read Darwin one Christmas.

"Here it is." Artie placed a heavy green, gold-embossed volume in my hand. "The color pictures are in the middle."

I set the book on Uncle Henry's desk and opened it slowly.

The pictures were terrible and marvelous—all at once. Each picture spread across two pages with a piece of tissue in between. In one, a huge green monster chased an armored lizardlike thing through a swamp. On the next page, a tall, long-necked yellow creature guarded a placid lake. I looked up at Artie.

"What does Uncle Henry think? Were these animals ever alive?"

Artie's lips tightened. "Dad believes in them."

"Do you?"

"I guess so. You can't argue with skeletons, and Dad saw one when he was back in New York this summer."

I pulled the newspaper article out of my pocket. "Let's see what the newspaper says."

My hands trembled as I unfolded the article. Papa would say if you believed in dinosaurs, you couldn't believe in God.

"You know, Tabitha," Artie said softly, "they've got one of those monsters made out of corn over at the Corn Palace, at the main exhibition hall. A scientist from back East is going to lecture on dinosaurs this afternoon. Dad set the whole thing up."

"Why didn't you tell me?" I cried. But I was smiling. Maybe Artie hadn't changed. It was part of an old game we always played, setting each other up for a big surprise.

Artie shrugged. "I thought maybe you didn't care about science anymore. Most girls don't when they're almost sixteen."

"Arthur Winslow, you should know me better than that!" I said, laughing.

"Okay, okay. But seriously," Artie said, lowering his voice, "your papa will be furious if you go. Dad thinks you should think this over carefully."

That was true. If I asked Papa's permission, he'd say no. And I'd never exactly deceived Papa before, although I made sure he didn't know the kind of books Uncle Henry sent home with me after our annual summer visits. But an opportunity like this didn't come along every day.

"This is something I have to do," I said finally.

"You'll catch hellfire." Artie's eyes twinkled.

I smiled and folded the article away in my pocket. Maybe Janette's hold on Artie wasn't as strong as I thought. I crossed to the door and opened it just a little. "Will you go with me?"

"Wouldn't miss it."

# Chapter 2

Aunt Eleanor's front parlor clock chimed the quarter hour, and up on the landing Artie gestured frantically, my hat and linen jacket on his arm. Silently he mouthed, "Let's go." I nodded from the parlor doorway and glanced over at Papa, who was stretched out on the sofa. A white handkerchief covered his face: Papa was having one of his headaches.

He lifted a finger and motioned me toward him. I would have to come up with some excuse for going out the whole afternoon. It really wasn't fair. My brother Stephen had just turned twelve; he could come and go as he pleased. I'd be sixteen in November, old enough for my teaching certificate. But no, I still had to ask Papa's permission for everything.

"Tabitha," he whispered, pulling the handkerchief aside, "tell your mother I'm going up to bed." He slowly got to his feet. "Run out to the kitchen and get me a cold compress."

I nodded solemnly, trying not to smile. This was

perfect. Papa would nap the whole afternoon away while Artie and I were at the lecture with Uncle Henry. He'd never even notice I was gone!

As Papa shuffled across the parlor, I backed into the doorway and signaled up to Artie. If he could just hide my jacket and hat behind his back . . .

"What are you doing, Tabitha Ruth!" Papa grabbed my arm. "I told you to go to the kitchen."

"Yes, Papa." I nodded up at Artie. But it was too late. Papa was already in the hall.

"Are you two going out, Arthur?" Papa didn't believe in nicknames.

"Well yes, sir, we are. Janette Becker invited us for a game of croquet, then sodas at her father's drugstore. Is that all right, Uncle Charles?"

I held my breath. You never knew how Papa would feel about even the most harmless occupations when we were under Uncle Henry and Aunt Eleanor's roof.

"That sounds fine, Arthur."

I sighed. It didn't even matter that Artie used Janette Becker as our excuse, I decided, crossing the kitchen. I glanced out the window and saw Mama and Aunt Eleanor in the garden, picking the season's last green beans.

"Papa's upstairs," I called from the back porch. "Artie and I are going out this afternoon."

"Have a good time, Tabitha," Mama called back. "Be home in time for supper."

I tiptoed up the back stairs with the damp cloth for Papa's forehead and pushed open the door. The room was dark and airless, with glimmers of sickly yellow light framing the pulled shades.

I put the cloth over Papa's head and turned to go. He caught my hand. "Thank you, Tabitha. Set a good example for your cousin and Miss Becker." He spoke softly, slowly, as he always did with a headache. It was almost as if his whole body had suddenly collapsed from the heavy burden of too many words, the weight of days and weeks of sermons.

I pulled my hand away.

"Be home by four," he whispered painfully. "Bible study. Be sure to tell your brother if you see him."

Bible study in Aunt Eleanor's parlor. Why did he make us do this? It was so embarrassing, so unnecessary. We never did it at home.

Almost as if he'd read my thoughts, Papa repeated, "Set a good example." He closed his eyes and turned his face toward the wall.

Out on the front porch, Artie handed me my hat and jacket and we ran to the corner.

"What took you so long?" he asked, pulling me through a dizzying crowd of people. But he didn't wait for my answer. There on the opposite side of the street was Janette Becker. She stood out even in a crowd. Short, blonde, and pleasantly plump, wearing an angelic white sporting costume of Italian linen, she looked like the pictures of fashionable ladies in Aunt Eleanor's latest issue of *Harper's Bazaar*.

"You going with us?" Artie asked, his hand still resting in the small of my back.

"How dreary," Janette pouted. "That stuffy old lecture hall and those beastly old beasts. Honestly, Tabitha, I don't understand how anyone could find such things so fascinating."

I glanced at Artie, who seemed mesmerized by the movement of Janette's mouth.

"We don't have much time," I said, glancing over my shoulder. "Are you coming or not?"

Janette linked her arm through Artie's. "Why don't I walk you to the Corn Palace, and then I'll decide."

There wasn't room for all three of us to walk arm in arm, so I dropped behind, letting Artie cut a path through all the people. They seemed to pour in from every side street, all streaming down Main toward the Corn Palace. Businessmen with thick, gold watch chains peeking from their vests. Fashionable-looking women in creamy summer wool walking costumes, their flat straw hats trimmed with ostrich feathers. But Uncle Henry said that all this was *nothing* compared to the cities back East with their art galleries, theaters, and museums. Museums where, Artie said, Uncle Henry had seen complete dinosaur skeletons that soared two or three stories high!

We rounded the corner and bumped into Stephen. His hands were sticky with licorice.

"Watch where you're going, young man." Janette straightened her skirt and frowned.

"Where are *you* going?" Stephen cocked his head and squinted.

My eyes met Artie's and I shook my head.

"I know you, Tabbie. You're going to hear that professor friend of Uncle Henry's. Probably believes we all descended from apes." Stephen waved "The Official Corn Palace Daily Programme" in my face and shook his head. "All I can say is, Papa better not find out."

I grabbed Stephen's arm, but he pulled away. "Then again, maybe you're not going," he smirked. "Miss Fancy Petticoat here couldn't sit through one of Papa's sermons, much less a discourse on the terrible lizards of the American West."

Stephen made a face, then dodged into the crowd.

"Stephen Fortune," I shouted. "Stephen! Come back here!"

"Don't worry, Tabbie, Stephen's a good kid. He won't tell on you." Artie put his arm around me and led me toward the Corn Palace gates.

I wasn't so sure. It would be just like Stephen to tell on me. He might be a good kid when it came to *his* friends or impressing people like Artie. But I knew how he liked to play me off against Papa. "Women are clearly the weaker sex," Stephen liked to say. It was a phrase he'd picked up from a circuit preacher who visited two winters ago and lectured on the "Evils of Women's Suffrage."

We stopped just outside the gates.

"Are you going or not?" Artie demanded, pressing Janette's arm.

"Well," Janette drawled, whirling her parasol and glancing at me. She batted her eyes and smiled so Artie would see the dimple in her right cheek.

I moved away, not really wanting to listen. Janette would flirt a little, I suspected, then decide to meet us later at her father's drugstore for sodas. But she'd keep Artie dangling for a few more agonizing seconds.

I looked up, up. I'd been here three days, but I could never get enough of the Corn Palace. A castle right here in the middle of town. Painted minarets pierced the sky like needles on a satin pincushion. Elaborate mosaics pieced together with corn, wheat, and grain formed giant pictures of important moments in American history: Washington crossing the Delaware; Lee and Grant at Appomattox; General Custer's discovery of gold in the Black Hills. Uncle Henry was right. This *was* a shrine to progress.

Suddenly Artie was at my elbow, pushing me through the gates.

"She's not coming," he mumbled. "We'll meet her later at the drugstore."

I resisted the urge to say "I told you so." If I had been a boy, I might have been just as mesmerized by Janette as Artie. Still, Artie should be more discriminating.

Inside, the Corn Palace was dark, the air stifling. It had turned hot this week, as it sometimes does in September, and the Corn Palace wasn't properly ventilated. I followed Artie through two long, high hallways. I'd already seen the exhibits there: "The Wonders of Modern Electricity" and "Amazing Feather Portraits of America's Great Men." Artie turned into a narrow passageway filled with people.

"I guess there are more people here than Dad planned for," he said over his shoulder.

"Didn't Uncle Henry expect a big crowd?"

"Not really. The terrible lizard lecture is up against Mr. Sousa's last concert and a real Sioux Indian wedding."

We squeezed through the last cluster of people gathered around the door, then pushed into the lecture hall.

Still, I couldn't see anything. Where was the terrible lizard sculpted from corn?

Suddenly the crowd parted, and there it was. A massive, square, pig-shaped creature, maybe thirty feet long, with a huge shield sweeping back over its head and three deadly horns protruding from its face. The shield and horns were fashioned from blood-red kernels of corn. Its body was studded with yellow, blue, and white kernels. The dinosaur held its head close to the ground, its mouth wide open, exposing daggerlike teeth of pearly white sculpted corn. I couldn't help being a little disappointed. I had hoped for one of those tall dinosaurs that stood erect on two legs.

Uncle Henry spotted us and motioned toward two front-row seats he had saved, then consulted his pocket watch. He moved toward the lectern, just to the left of the dinosaur's horns, which must have been at least three feet long.

"Ladies and gentlemen," he called out in his clear professor tone. Though a small man, Uncle Henry had a voice almost as big as Papa's.

"We are indeed privileged to have with us today a preeminent scholar in the relatively new science of vertebrate paleontology. An outstanding paleontologist in his own right, he has also studied at the feet of the master, the world-renowned Dr. O. C. Marsh." Uncle Henry paused dramatically and took off his reading glasses. "Our speaker today is a graduate of Yale University, where he is now a professor of paleontology. He has conducted massive excavations throughout our Great American West, and today he will reveal to you the tremendous secrets of a dark age. Ladies and gentlemen, I give you Dr. Phineas Parker, dinosaur hunter extraordinaire!"

# Chapter 3

Dr. Phineas Parker emerged from the shadows behind the corn dinosaur and bowed to the cheering crowd. He was short, like Uncle Henry, but stout. His vest stretched across his ample stomach and held him in like a corset. Somehow I'd expected a dinosaur hunter to be tall and lean and rugged.

"Imagine, if you will, ladies and gentlemen, a giant primeval jungle," Dr. Parker said. His voice was just barely a whisper, but it carried, like Papa's, out into the crowd. I shifted forward in my seat.

"You see thick, tangled undergrowth," he continued. "Tall, towering trees. In the distance, an angry red volcano belches fire."

His words formed a picture like one of Papa's sermons about hellfire and brimstone, but this time I was there, seeing what Dr. Parker wanted me to see.

"You move in closer," he coaxed. "Unseen. Invisible. Looking at a world no human eyes have ever penetrated."

Dr. Parker paused, and I paused with him, waiting

for something gigantic and marvelous. Then his voice rose like the crest of a giant wave.

"Suddenly you hear a terrifying sound, like nothing you've heard before. The ground shakes, and there ahead in the clearing you see *Triceratops*, the great armored lizard of the late Cretaceous period."

I whispered *Triceratops* and liked the sound of it.

"There he is!" Dr. Parker gestured grandly toward the corn dinosaur. "Close to the jungle floor!"

In that instant I forgot that the creature in front of me was made of corn. It was as if Dr. Parker had magically transformed it into a living, breathing animal, as real as Artie sitting next to me.

"He bellows in rage," Dr. Parker cried, "and his tremendous horns rip through the stomach of his opponent—a giant meat-eater, three times his height."

The crowd murmured. A woman right behind me even screamed. But I felt no fear, only an insatiable curiosity.

Dr. Parker paused again. He smiled faintly, like Papa did when he held his audience in the palm of his hand. Once again, Dr. Parker lowered his voice to a dramatic whisper.

"But you and I, ladies and gentlemen—you and I are the only witnesses of this magnificent but beastly act of primitive nature. A struggle for survival in a world long past."

The entire hall broke into a round of cheers and applause. Artie clapped wildly; Uncle Henry smiled and nodded at the crowd. But I sat still, waiting to hear more, and wondering what Papa would say about a man as gifted as Dr. Parker. Could Dr. Parker persuade Papa to consider a world so different from Genesis? How could *anyone* doubt the existence of dinosaurs when Dr. Parker could bring them to life? I wanted to study with someone like him, to learn what he knew.

Dr. Parker held up his hands. "Thank you, thank you, ladies and gentlemen. But before I go on, I must congratulate your able Dakota artisans who have so cleverly wrought this creature of corn that serves as an inspiration to us all."

There were more cheers, more whistles.

"I can assure you, we have nothing like it at the Peabody Museum back at Yale!"

The crowd laughed and applauded, but I wondered if Dr. Parker's praise was genuine. There was something in his voice that reminded me of Papa's diplomacy after a bad Sunday dinner at Sister Porter's. "You shouldn't have gone to so much trouble," Papa would say. Back at Yale, Dr. Parker could run his fingers along a real *Triceratops* horn, could hold one of its teeth in his hand. Most of the people here today came to see nothing more than a life-sized toy made of corn.

"But, ladies and gentlemen," Dr. Parker said, lowering his voice, "I must confess, our knowledge about these creatures is sadly incomplete. There is so much we do not know about the terrible lizards that once ruled our earth."

Dr. Parker suddenly sounded earnest and genuine, almost personal. "Just twelve years ago, those of us working with Dr. Marsh had never seen or heard of *Triceratops*." He pointed to a map behind the dinosaur. "By chance one day, on the High Plains just east of the Rocky Mountain range, we came upon a fossil horn, all that remained of a tremendous ghost creature."

Ghost creature! The phrase took me back home to Rim, to Mama's friend, old Sally Dancing Moon. She used a phrase almost like Dr. Parker's. *Ghost horses*, she called them. At night in the Badlands, she said, the ghost horses came alive and flew from canyon to canyon, butte to butte. Silent, huge, and fierce. Her stories had given me terrifying but wonderful dreams, and for a long time, Papa wouldn't let me see her unless he or Mama was with me.

Dr. Parker's voice rose and fell, but I was miles away, in Sally's cabin. "Look for the bones of the ghost horses, Little One," she used to say. "They will teach you great mysteries." Could those bones that Sally talked about in the Badlands belong to dinosaurs?

I looked up at Dr. Parker, who surveyed his audience like Papa did right before he issued the invitation song at the end of Sunday-morning service.

"I ask today for your support. Because next spring," Dr. Parker said forcefully, "when we move closer to a new century, I'll be digging for dinosaurs once again.

On the other side of your great state, just east of the sacred Black Hills . . ."

My heart skipped a beat.

". . . on the Great Sioux Reservation, in the Badlands, just south of Rim."

I closed my eyes. All around me, everyone was on their feet. Cheering. Stomping. Whistling.

Dr. Parker was coming to Rim! To hunt dinosaurs! This was my chance!

He raised his hands and the crowd settled down.

"Now, ladies and gentlemen, may I field any questions?"

There was an awkward pause. Then suddenly the questions poured in.

"Did human beings live during the age of dinosaurs?"

"Were dinosaurs related to dragons?"

"Had the dinosaurs been killed during the great flood?"

"Why doesn't the Bible mention dinosaurs?"

No one asked about the Badlands expedition. Didn't anyone want to know about that? When would he be in Rim? What did he expect to find? Had he already surveyed the area? Those were the questions people should be asking.

I raised my hand.

"Yes, little lady?"

I stood up, aware of Artie next to me, aware suddenly of a room full of people. But that didn't matter.

"Will you be hiring assistants for your expedition next year?"

"Only a scout or two, my dear." Dr. Parker turned away and started to answer another question.

I cleared my throat and raised my voice. "But will there be opportunities for local students interested in the study of dinosaurs?"

Dr. Parker frowned. "The expedition to Rim will be a serious scientific endeavor. I'll have room only for the most seasoned and experienced assistants."

Artie grabbed my arm and pulled me down in my seat.

"I can't believe you asked that!"

"Why not? I really want to study with Dr. Parker."

Artie shook his head. "You? Tabbie, when are you going to grow up?"

I jerked my arm away. "I'm going to hunt dinosaurs with Dr. Parker next year. Just wait and see."

Artie shook his head again, and I knew then that something *was* different about him, something that went beyond an infatuation with Janette. He seemed hopeless, resigned to something.

The crowd was breaking up and a few people clustered around Dr. Parker and Uncle Henry.

"Come on," I said, taking Artie's arm. "Let's get your dad to introduce us."

"Only if you promise not to say anything foolish," Artie warned.

We stood just behind the corn *Triceratops*, waiting for Uncle Henry and Dr. Parker to exit through the back entrance of the lecture hall. Finally, they turned our way.

"Ah, Phineas, let me introduce my son Arthur and my niece Tabitha Fortune. Tabitha's family lives in Rim. Her father is a kind of missionary to the Indians there."

Dr. Parker nodded and took my hand. "A delightful little lady, I'm sure."

I smiled back, wondering if he always called ladies "little." I was just as tall as Uncle Henry, Artie, *and* Dr. Parker.

He reached into a pocket and pulled out a thin ebony case. "Perhaps you'll be interested in seeing this, Miss Fortune." He snapped open the box. It held a fossil tooth, perhaps seven inches long.

"Terrifying, isn't it?" Dr. Parker asked, raising one eyebrow.

"It's fascinating," I whispered. He seemed disappointed when I asked, "May I take a closer look?"

Dr. Parker exchanged a glance with Uncle Henry.

"Tabitha is perfectly capable and reliable," my uncle said. "She's always been a gifted fossil-finder." His eyes smiled.

"Very well, Miss Fortune. You may hold it."

I hoped no one noticed how my hand shook as I reached for the tooth. It felt smooth and heavy in my hand. I turned it over slowly.

"Did it belong to your Triceratops?" I asked.

"No. It belongs to something else entirely. A carnivore—a meat-eater."

I handed the tooth back to Dr. Parker. "And you hope to find this carnivore in the Badlands?"

"Well, yes. Actually I do." He seemed surprised that I could jump to such a logical conclusion.

"Then you'll need a good scout, someone who knows the area well."

"Yes, I will. Perhaps your father could suggest someone," he returned.

I glanced over at Uncle Henry, who shook his head. Papa would never cooperate with someone like Dr. Parker. Nor would he ever let anyone in his family cooperate with him.

In my head, I heard old Sally's voice again. *"Ghost horses. They will teach you great mysteries."*

"I know the area very well myself," I said suddenly.

Artie snorted. Uncle Henry raised his eyebrows.

"What?" Dr. Parker chuckled. "A delicate young lady like yourself?"

I smiled again, feeling Uncle Henry's gaze, trying to buy a little more time. I knew the Badlands better than Papa. Mama and I drove over them more often than he did, visiting reservation families. Why, our wagon had probably gone right by buried ghost horses hundreds of times!

"Vertebrate paleontology is no place for a lady, Miss Fortune, although I appreciate your interest." Dr. Parker turned to go.

*No place for a lady!*

I couldn't lose this chance. I glanced over at Artie. We were just about the same size. I was tall, willowy (*skinny*, my brother Stephen said). I'd always been a good rider. With my hair up under a hat . . .

"Wait, Dr. Parker."

He and Uncle Henry stopped in the doorway.

"Of course, you're right. The Badlands are no place for a lady, and I can only imagine the privations of an expedition." I paused. "But my brother is even more gifted than I am."

"Indeed?" Dr. Parker turned slowly.

"Yes. His scientific paper on Darwin won the Mantell Award for Student Achievement." That, at least, was partially true. I had won the competition—not Stephen.

"Your brother, Miss Fortune?"

"Yes, Dr. Parker. My brother." I took a deep breath and smiled. "My *twin* brother, Tom. Tom Fortune."

# *Chapter* 4

Dr. Parker handed me his card. "Have your brother write or cable me when you return to Rim, young lady. There's a great deal of work to do right away."

I nodded and bowed my head, trying to hide the anxious feelings racing up from my stomach, across my shoulders, and down my spine. I knew Uncle Henry and Artie were staring at me, but neither of them said a word.

"Now, if you'll excuse me, I think I have just enough time to catch the final performance of those Golden Girls." Dr. Parker shook my hand and rushed toward the back door. "Coming, Henry?"

"No, I'll meet you later at the Faculty Club," Uncle Henry said slowly. Then he took my elbow and led me out into the hall. "I need a smoke," he whispered.

Still holding my elbow, Uncle Henry cut a path through the crowds outside the Corn Palace. Artie, who still hadn't said anything, followed.

We crossed Main and reached campus in minutes. As we climbed the stairs to Uncle Henry's office, I wondered what it would be like to study at a real university, Princeton or Yale, where scholars examined *Triceratops* fossils in modern laboratories. That's what I really wanted. An expedition in the Badlands would give me a start and let me prove myself to an expert like Dr. Parker. Surely Uncle Henry and Artie could understand that.

Uncle Henry closed the door to his office, a big room with high ceilings and tall windows that looked out over campus. You could even see the blue, yellow, and red spires of the Corn Palace.

"Uncle Henry," I began, glancing at Artie, hoping for encouragement. He hovered by the door, spinning Uncle Henry's Great Globe of the Cosmos.

Uncle Henry held up his hands to silence me and reached for a cigar, then leaned back in the chair behind his desk. He looked out the window and inhaled deeply.

Finally he said, "How do you propose to do this, Tabitha? And how can I let you? Even if your father believed as I do, I couldn't let you go tramping off into the Badlands disguised as a boy."

He tapped his cigar against the edge of a giant brass ashtray and waved off my protests. "I know, Tabitha. Only your mother, or the Indians themselves, know the Badlands better than you. But, Niece, have you fully considered the matter? And with Parker, no less!"

"What do you mean by that?"

Uncle Henry settled back in his chair and smiled.

"Parker's a confirmed bachelor. Believes women should stay at home, be contented with learning a little about music and a lot about housekeeping." Uncle Henry turned and looked at me squarely. "According to Parker, that's the ideal extent of a young woman's education."

"Sounds like Papa."

I glanced back at Artie, again hoping for moral support. But he just stared at the spinning globe.

I turned away and gazed out the window. Was it hopeless then? I had no idea how to be Tom Fortune, how to join Dr. Parker in the Badlands without Papa's knowledge, or exactly where to scout for dinosaurs. Would I even recognize a dinosaur bone if I saw one? After all, I'd lived near the Badlands for seven years without realizing what was buried out there.

"Tabbie," Artie said at last, "you're in way over your head this time." The globe of the cosmos made a soft whirring noise. "We're not kids anymore. Face facts. What is it your papa always quotes from the Bible? 'When I became a man, I put away childish things.' "

"Don't quote Scripture to me, Artie Winslow!" I shouted. "I'm not being childish. This is something I want to do, something I *have* to do." My whole body was shaking. "What's happened to you, Artie? What's happened to all your dreams?"

Artie stopped spinning Uncle Henry's globe. His face was suddenly white and his voice shook. "I've become a realist, Tabbie. I'm not even going to college! I'm going to apprentice with Janette's father at the pharmacy."

I looked at Uncle Henry, who nodded. "Artie," I whispered, "why?"

"You have to grow up sometime," Artie shouted back, then whirled and ran out into the hall.

I stood by the window, breathing hard, fighting back tears. I could stand anything, *anything*, except this. All those summers here, picking up arrowheads and fossils. The nights in the porch swing talking about college—Yale or Princeton or wherever we chose to go.

From the window, I watched Artie as he darted out of the building, then across campus toward Main Street, toward Becker Drug Emporium, toward Janette.

"You won't help me either, will you, Uncle Henry," I said quietly, not wanting to face him.

"Tabitha, Artie made his own decision. He applied unsuccessfully at several universities back East. He couldn't even meet the standards to get into school here." Uncle Henry placed his arms on my shoulders. "He doesn't have your drive or determination—or your academic ability."

I knew how much it pained him to say that.

"Have I been childish?"

For a long moment, he was silent. The smoke from his cigar hung heavily in the air. Then Uncle Henry lifted my chin and I looked into those blue eyes I'd loved since I was a little girl.

"No," he said quietly. "You've only been impetuous. But you're right. You *should* dig for dinosaurs with Parker next summer. Maybe it's time your father—and Parker himself—learned that young women can do more than play the piano and fry chicken." He paused. "Let's go home, Tabbie. Or should I say, Tom?"

# Chapter 5

We walked back to the house together, and the sun cast long shadows across our path. Uncle Henry promised to send me a trunk full of books on anatomy, geology and (of course) dinosaurs. It would be heavy reading for the winter, but if I passed my teaching exam and accepted the post at White River School for the winter term, I could board with the Gilfillans and be well away from Papa, who'd never know what I was reading.

Then, too, I could put a little money aside to outfit myself for the Badlands. Most of my earnings would go back to Mama and Papa, since the big church in Kentucky had cut Papa's salary a little. But when Papa had finally agreed to the idea of my teaching, he'd also said I could keep part of the money.

"I don't like the idea of a disguise," Uncle Henry said, shaking his head as we elbowed our way through the Corn Palace crowd. "But I suppose it would be necessary, at least in the beginning."

I stepped through the shadow of a minaret. "Once I

gain Dr. Parker's confidence," I promised, "then I'll tell him who I really am."

"I'm very concerned with living conditions. A young girl alone . . ." Uncle Henry's voice trailed off. "How do I put this delicately?"

"You mean," I asked, "how will I live alone among all those men?"

"Precisely."

"I'll come up with a plan, Uncle Henry. Don't worry."

"But what about your father?" Then he whispered, almost to himself, "Maybe you should confide in your mother. Have you thought of that?"

"Mama?" I glanced at Uncle Henry. "I don't think so." Mama would never keep a secret from Papa.

We turned the last corner and Uncle Henry reached into his vest for his pocket watch. He clicked it open.

"Perfect timing. Eleanor should be putting the roast on the table just about now."

Dinnertime! I was supposed to be home by four. I'd forgotten Papa's devotional! I looked up at the sky. The long shadows. "What time is it?"

"It's almost six."

I broke away from Uncle Henry and ran up the street. Uncle Henry and Aunt Eleanor's buggy was parked in front of the house, and I could see our trunks out on the porch. Stephen lounged by the front gate, looking out for me.

"She's here!" he called, running back into the house. "She's here, Papa!"

The screen door swung open and Papa came out, his face dark with rage.

"Where have you been, girl?" he demanded.

"I've been with Uncle Henry and Artie. Papa, I'm sorry I forgot—"

"You've been to *the devil!*" Papa shook me hard. "An evolutionist lecture."

I pulled away and glared at Stephen.

"Be sure your sins will find you out," Stephen quipped, smirking from the doorway.

Uncle Henry bustled through the gate and put his arm around me. "What's going on here, Charles?"

"I'm taking my family away from this heathen citadel"—Papa motioned for Stephen to load the trunks—"before you further pollute the impressionable mind of my daughter."

Mama brushed past Stephen, her cheeks flushed, carrying a carpetbag and my satchel. Aunt Eleanor was right behind her.

"Don't be a fool, Charles," said Uncle Henry, still hugging me close.

"Say your good-byes," Papa ordered. "We won't be back again."

He pulled me away from Uncle Henry and shoved me toward the buggy. Mama hugged Aunt Eleanor, then climbed in beside me. Papa placed the last trunk in the back and took the reins from Stephen.

"We'll leave your buggy at the depot," Papa said.

Then he clucked to the horses and we were off.

# Chapter 6

" '"Unto the woman he said, "I will greatly multiply thy sorrow," ' " Papa read over the clatter of the tracks.

I sat straight in my seat, eyes closed, feeling his eyes boring into me. Papa and Stephen were on one side facing Mama and me on the other, our luggage crammed around our feet.

Papa and Stephen had started reading the night before, just after the train had pulled out of Mitchell. They droned on like the nightmare voices you hear just before a fever breaks. Finally, at Plankinton, they stopped—but only because it was too dark to read.

After that, I slept fitfully. Waking at every stop; banging against the hard, lumpy seat; seeing a jumble of images when I closed my eyes: the *Triceratops* of corn; Janette's creamy white skin, her puffed sleeves; Artie, dashing across campus toward his future.

Just after dawn, Papa and Stephen started reading again. Papa chose the readings deliberately. All of them were about sin and damnation. All of them were for *my* benefit. To properly restore my soul to the will of God.

" 'In sorrow thou shalt bring forth children.' " Papa had this part memorized. " 'And thy desire shall be to thy husband, and he shall rule over thee.' "

It was one of Papa's favorite verses, and he had quoted it to me often during the last year—any time I mentioned college. "A woman of God," he would say, "belongs at the side of a righteous man. Pray for a godly husband, not a godless education."

Stephen read the next verse, and Mama reached for her valise. Uncle Henry's advice to confide in her flickered across my mind, and I wondered if she had ever desired more than a husband.

I squinted through partially opened eyes. Mama was counting her money. If we'd left the following Wednesday as planned, Aunt Eleanor would have sent us home with a basket of bread, fruit, and cheese for breakfast. Now we'd have to eat at a café during our two-hour stop in Pierre. I knew Mama was worried about café prices. Pierre was the state capital and it was expensive. How had Mama endured Papa's unreasonable behavior all these years?

" 'And the Lord God said,' " Papa read as Stephen passed the Bible back, " ' "Behold, the man is become as one of us, to know good and evil . . ." ' "

Papa was coming to his favorite part, which he always read in his best fire-and-brimstone voice, especially when he was angry with me. He expected me to feel ashamed of myself. He expected me to be afraid of dying and going to hell. But I wasn't afraid, so I looked straight at him, unblinking.

Papa's voice boomed, " 'Therefore—' "

Suddenly the conductor moved down the aisle yelling, "Pierre. Pierre, South Dakota!"

Mama lightly touched Papa's hand and shook her head, holding her finger to her lips. She hated scenes as much as I did.

People all around us were getting up, collecting their bags, but Papa's voice boomed out again, " 'Therefore, the Lord God sent him forth from the garden of Eden!' "

Papa lowered his voice and leaned forward. " 'So he drove out the man . . .' "

He closed the Bible and repeated, " 'He *drove out* the man.' "

Then he roared, "Beware, Tabitha, lest you be driven out likewise!"

I felt blood rush to my cheeks, conscious of an aisleful of strangers. A Norwegian family crammed in the row ahead of us turned to stare. Stephen smirked. He always liked it when Papa preached at me, especially in public.

"Lest you be driven out," Papa continued, "in your thirst for forbidden knowledge."

Even the conductor was watching me now. How could Papa do this? Nothing I had done, nothing I would ever do deserved *this* kind of punishment!

"It is the curse of the weaker sex," Papa said, his eyes wild and fierce, "to desire that which is forbidden. The inheritance of Eve! The curse of Eve!" He lowered his voice to a whisper. "And you're just like her, Tabitha. Craving forbidden fruit, craving knowledge that belongs only to the Eternal!"

I leaned forward and looked right at Papa. "I'd rather commit a sin like Eve than blame my curiosity on someone else—like Adam did," I snapped.

His hand rose to strike me, but Mama was faster. She caught his wrist and held it firmly.

"That's quite enough, Charles," she said, getting to her feet and moving into the aisle. "Come, Tabitha. Let's find the ladies lounge."

Breathing hard, shaking, I reached for my satchel. I glanced over at Stephen, who for once looked scared, *really* scared. I looked back at Papa, his face now white and pasty, then followed Mama off the train.

The morning air felt cool and fresh against my cheeks. I suddenly felt strong and sure of myself, eager to take control of my life *now*. What if I decided not to get back on the train? I looked up the hill where the new capitol building was supposed to be built. This was a prosperous place. Surely I could find something to do, earn my fare back to Mitchell, and enroll at Dakota Wesleyan with Uncle Henry. I didn't care if I ever saw Papa again.

For an instant, I considered it.

Then I considered what I would lose: the opportunity to study with Dr. Parker, to uncover the ghost horses that lay buried in my own Badlands. True, it was a whole winter away, and I had no idea how I would become Tom Fortune and lead Dr. Parker's party to dinosaur bones. But I would find a way, regardless of Papa. *Because* of Papa.

I turned and followed Mama across the platform, through a powder-blue door marked Pierre Ladies Lounge. It was a small, dingy room with a few pieces of shabby furniture, a cloudy mirror, a wash basin, tepid water, and a chamber pot.

"It isn't prudent to incite your father, Tabitha," Mama said, taking her best mother-of-pearl hat pin from the brim of her velvet-banded straw. "You must be more cautious in the future. He can be a difficult man, especially when confronted with things he can't understand."

*"Maybe you should confide in your mother . . ."*

I took off my hat slowly, watching Mama's reflection in the mirror.

Her hand brushed my cheek. "You have so much to learn, Daughter." Then she reached for the brush in her valise and loosened the pins in my hair.

We pulled away from the platform four hours late, hungry again because we had money enough only for breakfast. A relentless white heat bore down on the train like a blast from Babylon's fiery furnace. I looked out the open window. Brown unbroken plains pitched toward an endless, cloudless sky. A herd of pronghorn kicked up bursts of dust against the horizon, and I envied their freedom.

"We will speak no more of what happened in Mitch-ell," Papa said suddenly, opening his Bible. "But we will forever remember its lessons." His voice shook a little.

Mama must have cornered him in the café and told him he'd been too hard on me this time. Still, I expected extended readings from Revelation about the end of the world and what happens to the unrepentant. So I turned back to the window.

"We will forever remember its lessons," Papa repeated sternly. He passed me his Bible. It was opened to First Corinthians 13, Apostle Paul's chapter on charity. "You read now, Tabitha Ruth." His voice was firm. "It will soothe our minds and hearts and turn our thoughts to peace."

I knew this was as close as Papa would ever come to an apology, so I began to read. But I couldn't forgive him.

The train pulled into Rim at sundown. Nobody was there to meet us because nobody knew we were coming; we weren't expected until Wednesday. Stephen ran over to Luke's Livery and got a wagon for our trunks. Mama and I walked home alone, down the wide, dusty street, just a block long. Papa and Stephen loaded the wagon.

There wasn't much to Rim—just a few storefronts, the Presbyterian Church (Papa's church met in the back of Mr. Knudson's Hardware), the school, and a cluster of little gray houses. But when you looked south, just off our front porch, you could see the spires of the Badlands, not five miles away. I stood there with Mama as she unlocked the front door. The Badlands were twisted, rocky shadows against a blood-red sky.

"Hell with the fires burned out"—that's what the first explorers had called them.

"Come inside, Tabitha," Mama said from the doorway, a lighted kerosene lamp in her hand.

I turned for one last look at the Badlands against the crimson sky. There were ghost horses out there, and I heard them calling to me.

# Chapter 7

"So yer gonna pretend to be a boy and ride out with a passel a book-smart swells lookin' fer bones a dead critters." Abby Hart shook her head and blew smoke rings at the ceiling. Except for Papa, people out here didn't make much of a fuss about Abby's cigars. She ran the post office and Western Union too efficiently for that.

Abby tapped her cigar and flakes of ash made a little mound on the counter. I couldn't tell if she was disgusted or impressed. You never could with Abby. She was hard and tough and stringy, like the fried chicken at Sister Porter's. But I wanted her approval—and needed it. Abby Hart was the only person in Rim who could help me create Tom Fortune.

At last she snuffed out her cigar and nodded her head. "I can see the romance in that. Sure, I'll send a telegram fer ya, and hold any that come in fer Mr. Tom Fortune. Now what do ya want to say to this here Dr. Parker?"

She pulled out a slip of paper printed WESTERN UNION and licked the end of her pencil.

"I think I need to write this out for myself first," I said. "Could I have a sheet of paper?"

She grunted and reached for the tablet under the counter. I knew Abby hated indecision: that's why she had taken over the post office two years ago. Her son Jesse was the official postmaster, but he wasn't very good at it.

I stared at the blank piece of paper. Something decisive, quick, intelligent. That's how this telegram needed to be. "Dr. Parker," I wrote, glancing up at Abby.

She sorted a stack of letters, holding each one up to the light before putting it in its proper box. Abby knew everything about everybody, which was fine if she liked you.

I scratched out the line I'd just written to Dr. Parker. Too long. Telegrams had to be short.

The bell over the door jingled and Mr. Knudson came in with a package under his arm. I moved out of the way and laid my left hand across what I had written.

"Mornin', Abby. Mornin', Tabitha," he said, handing the package to Abby.

"Won't go out till Monday, Homer," she said. "Ya missed the eleven-thirty."

Mr. Knudson took out his pocket watch. "It's just now ten o'clock."

"Left early today," Abby grunted.

Mr. Knudson scowled at Abby. "I'll be back Monday mornin' then. Bright and *early*." He stuffed his parcel back under his arm and moved toward me. "What's that you're workin' on, Tabitha?"

"A shopping list for Mama," I said quickly, hiding the line I'd just written. Mr. Knudson came to church regularly (he felt he should since it met in his store), but he wasn't really a member. Still, I couldn't afford to arouse suspicion.

"Heard you saw some mighty interestin' things East River," he said, still looking over my shoulder.

I nodded.

"Golden Girls—and all that," he whispered, looking at me hopefully.

"I didn't see them," I said, still hiding Dr. Parker's name across the top of the tablet.

"Too bad." Mr. Knudson paused. "But I'm looking forward to tomorrow's sermon." He paused again. "Reckon your pa will mention those Golden Girls?"

"I really couldn't say." I laughed, relieved that Mr. Knudson was far more interested in the Golden Girls than my "shopping list."

"See you in church," he said, reaching for the door. Then he glanced back at Abby. "Wouldn't hurt you none, Abby Hart, to grace a pew now and again."

"I'd have more 'n Golden Girls on my mind ifen I did," Abby retorted.

Mr. Knudson snorted and slammed the door.

Abby ground out her cigar. "You got that telegram ready yet?"

"How does this sound?" I paused. "Dr. Parker. Am interested in scouting for Badlands expedition. Write or wire with details, number in party, etc. Yours, Thomas Fortune."

Abby squinched up her eyes and stared at the ceiling. Her skin crinkled up in ridges. She ran her hands through her wiry, bobbed hair. From the neck up, Abby looked as much like a man as Mr. Knudson.

"Not good enough," she said finally. "Ya haven't asked about money."

"Money?"

"If yer gonna be a scout," she said, putting both hands down on the counter, "ya gotta get paid."

"But I just want to learn."

"That's what's wrong with you young ladies today. It's a cold, hard world out there, and ya gotta make your way in it somehow. Now the fellas, they've already got that figgered out. All of 'em, that is, 'cept my Jesse."

A salary! Yes, Abby was right. If I were going to be a boy—a young man, really—I'd have to make demands like one. "How much do you think I should ask for?"

I had no doubt Abby would know. She'd done so much—been a bull whacker with Calamity Jane between Fort Pierre and the Black Hills, homesteaded on her own up in Wyoming. Some people said she had even voted for Grover Cleveland before she moved in with Jesse three years before.

"Tabitha," she said, relighting her cigar, "I reckon

ya don't need to ask fer anything. Here, why don't ya say sompum like this." Abby squinted again and cocked her head to one side. "Dr. Parker. If price is right, will scout for Badlands expedition. Wire immediately with offer and details."

"That sounds good."

Abby nodded, then pursed her lips. "Wonder if he needs a good camp cook. Most of these fellers do, ya know."

"Camp cook?"

"I wouldn't mind getting in on the action myself. Feelin' cooped up here. Too civilized." Abby blew smoke rings at the ceiling. "What'd ya say to that, Tabbie Girl?"

I looked out the window. Mr. Knudson and Stephen stood out in the street, probably talking about Ernie Jones's Golden Girls. The Lowry brothers from Bad River Ranch were loading up their buckboard with supplies. They stopped to listen to Stephen, who gestured suggestively with his hands. No doubt about it. He was definitely describing the Golden Girls down to the last pearl on their costumes.

I needed more than an ally, I decided then. I needed a coconspirator, somebody who was wise and smart and understood the way men thought. The way men behaved. Maybe Abby was on to something.

"I think that could be a *very* good idea, Abby. But let's wait till I hear back from Dr. Parker. Tom Fortune shouldn't be too eager to help just yet."

Abby nodded. "That's the way to think, Tabbie. Like a man. Get your offer first, *then* go to work."

I reached into my pocket for the spending money I'd saved from winning last spring's Mantell Award. I wasn't sure how much it cost to wire Yale University.

"Send the telegram," I said, laying two silver dollars on the counter, "the way you wrote it."

"Laws, girl! You could buy the whole place for two dollars—includin' Jesse!" Then Abby leaned across the counter and whispered, "Besides, this one's on me. No charge."

# Chapter 8

Stephen had drawn quite a crowd—mostly men—in front of Mr. Knudson's Hardware.

"There was one dancer," I heard him say, "with legs up to here, who moved like a wildcat."

The Lowry brothers whistled, and I wondered if they'd be in church the next day. If Stephen kept this up, Papa would probably draw quite a crowd—men *and* women—expecting to hear about the "Evils of Lewd Dancing in Public Places."

I stopped under a big cottonwood, the only one in town, and looked up the short street toward home. Our house was so small. Two bedrooms, a kitchen that doubled as a sitting room, and a lean-to off the back that Papa called the study. Stephen slept up under the eaves in the loft.

I always hated coming home to Rim after a trip to Uncle Henry and Aunt Eleanor's. Their house always made ours feel so sad and confining. A place without books. A place without freedom.

Papa stood out on our narrow front porch, a glass of

iced tea in his hand. "I must put my shoulder to the plow, Dorothy," he boomed, as Mama joined him. "The fields are ripe unto harvest, and the kingdom of God is at hand." He looked out toward the Badlands, then back at Mama.

She motioned for me to come home.

Papa lowered his voice. "I've tried to put the evils of Mitchell behind me, but I cannot. Too much is at stake."

I could feel Papa staring at me, then he went inside and shut himself up in the study. We didn't see him for the rest of the day. Mama took him a sandwich and more iced tea on a tray at lunchtime. He refused to eat supper.

But we heard him. Practicing. Reading fragments of verses and phrases out loud as he wrote. He didn't come to bed until late. Alone in my room, with the window open and the crickets singing their late summer song, I suspected Papa's sermon wouldn't be about Ernie Jones's Golden Girls. It would be about dinosaurs.

And maybe about me.


Stephen and Papa left early for church to set out the wooden folding chairs in front of the counter at Knudson's. It was also Stephen's job to hang sheets in the stockroom to divide the Sunday school classes—one for very young children, the other for older boys. The boys' class practiced reading from the Scriptures, praying aloud, and leading the singing. Singing was important because the church was too poor to have a piano.

There wasn't a class for older girls.

Mama and I taught the class for little children, and usually left early for services, too. But today we lingered at home just a few more minutes. Sister Porter had volunteered to take the class—if, she said, enough children showed up.

"Tabitha, are you ready?" Mama called from the kitchen.

I pinned on my hat and looked at my reflection in the mirror. How would it feel to be the inspiration for a sermon? I had never directly inspired one of Papa's sermons before, though I knew plenty of other people who had. Mr. Knudson, for one, who was always at church on Sundays but had never been baptized. And Brother Porter's oldest son, who baled hay on Sundays. Even Sister Cotton, who sometimes slipped out of church early to start her Sunday roast. Of course, Papa never named names. But everyone knew who he was talking about.

"Tabitha. We can't be late."

Well, it couldn't be worse than what had happened on the train. Besides, the people here knew me. Papa would have a hard time convincing anyone here that I was another Eve.

But I wondered what Papa would say about dinosaurs. He didn't know anything about them except what he might have read in the Mitchell *Daily Repub-*

*lican.* I suspected most folks would be disappointed with his sermon. For them, dinosaurs weren't nearly as fascinating as Golden Girls.

"Tabitha."

Mama leaned against the doorway, clasping her worn white leather Bible. She was wearing a new pair of pale salmon gloves, a gift from Aunt Eleanor. Papa wouldn't like that. And suddenly I wondered if Mama had chosen to wear them deliberately.

"Let's go," she whispered.

All the regulars were already there. But so were lots of other people—half the members of the Presbyterian Church from across the street, including Mr. Timothy, the schoolmaster. There must have been at least forty people crammed into Mr. Knudson's store—between plow blades, wagon wheels, and bags of seed. I didn't know Papa could draw a crowd like this!

"Your papa will be pleased," Mama whispered.

But I wondered, especially after Kitty Olson whispered in my ear, "Did you really see those Golden Girls dancing naked around the Maypole?"

As Mama and I inched through the crowd, I realized then that everyone was whispering about the Golden Girls, and everyone had his own story: The dancers wore transparent costumes of gold-spun gossamer; they coerced John Philip Sousa to play for them; they re-created the wicked Dance of Salome that had cost John the Baptist his head. In the stifling heat, Mr. Knudson and Willy File, the undertaker, passed out paper fans and shook their heads as the tales grew wilder and wilder.

"This is good for business," I heard Mr. Knudson whisper.

Finally Mama and I found two seats in the third row just as Brother Porter stood up behind the counter and cleared his throat.

"Usually we conduct . . . ah . . . Sunday school and . . . ah . . . Bible study before our regular church service." His voice quivered, his mouth sounded dry. Brother Porter had probably never addressed so many people before in his life. "But the Reverend Fortune . . . and the Brethren of this congregation have . . . ah . . . decided to cancel Sunday school . . . this morning. We don't want to keep you waiting in this heat for Reverend Fortune's . . . ah . . . fine sermon."

There were murmurs of approval all around. Clearly, everyone was eager to get to the Golden Girls.

Brother Porter cleared his throat again and in a quivering, high nasal tenor began to sing "A Mighty Fortress Is Our God."

He sang every verse.

Finally Papa stood up behind Mr. Knudson's counter. He held his Bible out high in his left hand and surveyed the congregation. " 'When I was child,' " he whispered dramatically, " 'I spake as a child, I understood as a child, I thought as a child: but when I became a man, I put away childish things.' "

First Corinthians 13—again! But today it made me

feel uncomfortable. It must have made everyone else uncomfortable, too. Cowboys shuffled in their seats. Wives glanced up at their husbands and shook their heads. This wasn't a promising beginning for a sermon on lewd dancing in public places.

"My family has just returned from the great Corn Palace Exposition in Mitchell, South Dakota," Papa still whispered. "And we saw many wondrous works of Man."

His voice rose as he glowingly listed all the exhibits and performances we'd seen. That surprised me, but it didn't please his audience.

Buck Lowry hollered from the back, "What about them Golden Girls, Preacher? They ain't no 'wondrous works of Man!' "

Papa paused. People shuffled in their seats. Uncomfortable. Maybe a little ashamed.

"My dear brothers and sisters in Christ," Papa thundered, "there's more of the Devil in the wondrous works of Man than in the sins of the flesh! Look back to the days of old. The Tower of Babel. The Kingdom of Babylon. Monuments to the Knowledge of Man. Monuments to Pride, Vanity, and Wickedness.

"And why are these more wicked?

"Think of Satan himself. The Angel who fell from Grace because he aspired to know the unknowable. The pleasures of the flesh are easy to recognize. The pleasures of the mind are more subtle. And thus, more beguiling."

Everyone shifted forward in their seats except me. And Mama.

"Deep in the heart of the Corn Palace," Papa whispered again, "the City of Mitchell erected an idol to the demon theory of evolution."

Several people in the crowd gasped, others squinted and shook their heads. I knew then that Papa was going to make evolution even more fascinating than lewd dancing.

I listened as he described the corn *Triceratops* in all its glory. Had Stephen provided the description? I looked over at Stephen. He winked and stuck out his tongue.

Papa got most of the important details about *Triceratops* wrong. It wasn't a gigantic meat-eater. It wasn't a great amphibian. Dr. Parker hadn't found it in the dark forests of northern Europe. It was so like Papa to get the facts wrong; he never researched a topic thoroughly.

"My friends, the Lord in his Great Wisdom has chosen to *confound* his enemies, those learned men who know not God, who crave forbidden knowledge."

My head began to pound. Papa raised his Bible higher.

"The Devil himself has left these so-called dinosaur bones, buried in the earth after the Great Flood, to mislead the minds of men and lure them to destruction! Oh Feebleminded Man," Papa roared, "to fall victim to the Devil's evil but childlike pranks!"

Dinosaur bones, planted by the Devil to mislead men of science!

That in itself was a "childlike" idea!

I couldn't even look at Papa. I was too embarrassed for him.

I thought of the tooth Dr. Parker carried in his pocket. The ghost horses waiting to be discovered in the Badlands. The Devil hadn't "planted" those bones. They were real. Dinosaurs were real. They had lived and breathed as surely as I sat in Rim, South Dakota, listening to Papa preach against them.

I glanced over at Mama. Her eyes were closed, her gloved hands clenched.

"Therefore, we must put away childish things," Papa whispered. "We must be diligent, believing *only* in the True Word of God." He leaned across the counter. "But we live in dangerous times. Satan's tricks are treacherous and full of guile. If the wise men of our day are tricked by Evil, how much easier is it then for sweet, impressionable youth—our very children—to be caught up in the passions of the day."

For a moment Papa looked straight at me. But I didn't flinch. Because Mama was holding my hand.

# Chapter 9

"I heerd I missed quite the sermon yesterday," Abby said from behind the Western Union window. "Your pa's got that Presbyterian preacher plum' jittery. Cuttin' in on his herd, so to speak."

I shrugged and closed the post office door behind me.

Everyone in town was talking about Papa's sermon and the "idol to the demon evolution," which was easier to pronounce than *Triceratops*. Papa was already planning his next sermon—on Ernie Jones's Golden Girls. But I had also noticed a new glimmer in people's eyes when I passed them on the street.

"Heerd you caused quite a stir yourself," Abby continued, opening a mailbag. "Not jist the obedient preacher's kid. You've got a reputation now."

"Like you?" I laughed.

"Maybe better." She snickered. "Jist wait till they find out what ya *really* have planned." Abby reached across the counter. "Here. There's a letter fer ya."

I stared at the envelope, BECKER DRUG EMPORIUM imprinted in black flourishes. My hand trembled.

"Not bad news, I hope."

"It's from my cousin Artie in Mitchell."

"I knew that," Abby said, reaching for a cigar.

"We had kind of an argument before Papa brought us home."

"Not surprised," she said, inhaling deeply. "Young fellers 'bout Artie's age git odd notions in their heads. They git worse, too, as they git older."

I skimmed the letter quickly.

Dear Tabbie:

I'm awfully sorry about what happened last week. Things have changed for me pretty fast and I'm not the person I used to be. It was hard for me to explain that to you because you haven't changed. You probably never will, probably never should.

Dad and I talked about your plans for working with Dr. Parker next summer. I wish you all the best. If anyone can pull it off, it's you.

Dad plans to send you a box of books at Christmas, and I'll send you some of my clothes if you like. That way if you get the job at White River, your earnings can go to more important things like buying yourself a revolver and renting a good horse.

I like my work here. Mr. Becker is not a bad

sort. Neither is Janette. You just need to give her a chance.

Write to me if you can.

Artie

I folded the letter and stuck it in my pocket.

"So what's he got to say fer hisself?" Abby asked.

"He apologized." I shrugged, not really wanting to talk about it. I was glad Artie was behind me again, but I felt sad for him. Somehow I just couldn't see Artie stuck behind a pharmacist's window.

"Is Mama's Kentucky package here?" I asked, wanting to change the subject.

Abby peered over a stack of boxes in the back. I knew my answer about Artie hadn't satisfied her, but Abby knew when to pry and when not to.

"Sure thing," she said, handing me a medium-sized box. "Came in this mornin'. You and your ma headed out to ole Sally's then?"

"Just me—and Stephen."

"Hmmmph. Jist you, ya mean. That brother of yourn, he'll find some way to skip off on his own today. You mark my words." She shook a crooked finger at me.

"I'd rather go by myself anyway."

I nodded good-bye and the door jingled behind me. Stephen had hired Old Gray and Crow from Luke's Livery. They were tied up out front when I got home. Mama opened the box and laid out the supplies she wanted us to take to Sally Dancing Moon. Two lengths of flannel, another of gray serge, and a small case of eyedrops we could only get from back East.

"Let's send this salt pork and cornmeal along, too," Mama said, making more room in the picnic hamper. "It may be winter before any of us gets back out there again. That's not too much for you to handle, is it, Tabitha?"

When Mama didn't go herself, she always put me in charge of delivering supplies. They came fairly regularly from the big church in Kentucky that supported us. Even though Papa's preaching to the Indians had failed, Mama had convinced the elders to support a few families on the reservation. The elders believed that, like Felix in the New Testament, the Indians— fed and clothed with Mama's supplies—would send for Papa "in a more convenient season" and respond to the Message of God. But their support only went so far; Mama paid for Sally's eyedrops herself.

"Be careful, children," Papa said, as I climbed into the saddle. "Protect your sister, Stephen," he added, handing him the shotgun and going back inside.

Shielding her eyes from the sun, Mama looked at me. "Tell Sally I'll try to see her before winter sets in. Tell her," she paused and almost whispered, "tell her I need that old box of papers. Bring it back with you."

Just beyond the first shallow ridge of sandstone cliffs, we met Billy Porter and two other boys.

"We're going swimming over at the stock pond. You coming, Steve?"

"You don't mind do you, Sis?" Stephen grinned. "You know the way to old Sally's blindfolded."

That was true, and I'd rather ride out by myself. It would give me a chance to talk to Sally about her ghost horses. But I said, "Don't you think it's a little cold for that?" The heat had broken the night before, and it was as cool as a morning in October. I didn't want to make things *too* easy for Stephen.

"Come on, Sis. You don't want me to go anyway."

"You owe me a favor, then. And I can call for it any time."

"Sure, sure."

"Give me the shotgun."

"Expectin' trouble from the natives?" Billy sneered.

"Bobcats, you idiot," I said, strapping the gun to my saddle. Papa didn't know I could shoot straight, but Artie had taught me years ago. I was a better shot than Stephen. A better rider, too.

"Meet you back here around five o'clock, Tabbie," Stephen called, as he and the boys galloped toward the stock pond.

"Remember. You owe me one!"

The sun was high overhead when I reached Sally's. She lived on a high ridge overlooking a rocky expanse of jagged Badlands spires. But up here the plain was grassy, broken by occasional sandstone outcroppings and a cluster of ponderosa pine.

Sally sat outside in a rickety chair, halfway between her sod-roofed hut and her dead husband's tipi.

"I've been waiting for you," she said, as I swung from Crow's saddle.

"I hope you haven't been waiting too long." I smiled. Sally always claimed she knew in advance when someone was coming to see her. I untied Mama's hamper from the saddle horn. "I brought lunch."

"What else did you bring?" she asked, still sitting motionless in the chair, a blanket around her shoulders. How frail she looked today, old and stooped.

I laid the lengths of plaid flannel across her lap.

"Ugly colors," she said. Sally ran her hands along the material. "Coarse, too."

"I brought salt pork and cornmeal."

"No bugs in it this time?"

I tried not to smile. Sally was never contented with anything Mama and I brought.

"And your eyedrops." I took the case of medicine inside and opened the wooden cabinet Mama had given Sally three years before. It was filled with unused bottles of eyedrops.

"Why aren't you taking your medicine, Sally?" I called from the front door.

"I see all I need to see."

I thought of Mama, scrimping and saving to pay for a whole case of expensive medicine. How could Sally be so thoughtless? I started outside, ready to give Sally the scolding she deserved, when I noticed a wooden box on the table. I picked it up carefully and carried it back into the sunshine.

"What's this?" I said, and laid the box in Sally's lap.

"It belongs to your mother." Sally's eyes narrowed in her round, leathery face. "It is time for you to have it."

I reached for the box, wanting to open it. But Sally was quicker. She placed it under her feet.

"We will talk of this later. Bring out a chair. I'm hungry."

You couldn't argue with Sally, but I could be stubborn, too. I filled a plate with cold fried chicken and handed it to her, without my usual small talk. I dragged out Sally's second chair and sat down beside her, munching on a chicken leg.

Sally turned away and stared out at the Badlands. Her fingers deftly picked the meat off a chicken wing. "Did you bring apple pie?"

I handed her the hamper. "See for yourself."

"It does not matter," she said, closing her eyes.

I looked out over the Badlands below us—a tangle of jagged, twisted peaks. "Tell me about ghost horses, Sally," I whispered.

Sally looked at me for a moment, then reached for the box under her feet. "We will talk of this now."

She handed me the box. It was perhaps ten inches long, eight inches wide, of what had once been smooth mahogany. Now it was battered and dirty, with nicks and gashes in its surface. It was unlocked and I lifted the hinged lid.

On the top there was a book, dark brown with gilded lettering. *An Authentic Collection of Sioux Folk Tales* by Mrs. Dorothy Stephens Fortune.

Dorothy Stephens Fortune! Mama? I opened the book and read the dedication. "To Mrs. Sally Dancing Moon, for her patience and guidance, and to my daughter, Tabitha."

For me—and Sally! Mama had dedicated her book to us. When had she published it? 1883. The year I was born. Why hadn't Mama told me about this? Why hadn't she written any more? Then I realized that Mama must have known Sally even before I was born, long before we moved to South Dakota.

I turned to ask Sally, but she had taken Mama's picnic hamper inside.

Underneath Mama's book were perhaps six volumes of slim science journals, *Scientific Thought for an Enlightened Age*. At the bottom of the box was a series of handmade maps—all of the Badlands, dating from 1892. I recognized Mama's handwriting. In the bottom right-hand corner, near the key, was the heading "1892 Badlands Expedition, Edward Drinker Cope." *Cope*. Where had I heard that name before?

"Good apple pie." Sally lowered herself back into the chair and nibbled on a piece of crust.

"How long have you known Mama?"

"My hair was as black as your pony's mane." Sally almost laughed and pointed to Crow with one thin gray braid. She took the box from my lap and nodded her head. "It is time that you should have this."

"But why? Why now?"

Sally gazed out at the Badlands. "It is a fine day. I am glad you chose it to come. But we will have an early winter. My grandson has seen the geese flying early."

She shook the box. "You be careful with this." She handed it back to me and rose. "It is time for you to go."

"But you haven't answered any of my questions."

"I have answered enough questions. I am tired."

I shook my head, knowing it was useless. Sally talked only when she wanted to. I carefully strapped Mama's box to the saddle and collected the hamper.

"I'll be back soon," I promised.

"Don't bother," Sally said, arms folded. "I'm going to my son's soon."

Still shaking my head, I turned Crow toward the trail.

"Come back in the spring," Sally called. She smiled broadly. "That will give you time to get used to your new name—One Who Goes Among Ghosts."

# *Chapter 10*

I rode to a secluded spot I knew, about a mile from Sally's, and tied Crow to a ponderosa pine. I took Mama's box of papers from the saddle and leaned against a boulder. I opened the box, setting Mama's book and the science journals aside. What interested me now were the maps.

I recognized most of the formations Mama had marked on the maps: Cedar Pass, Pinnacles, Sage Creek Butte. But four notations caught my eye. They were labeled Cretaceous, the era when Dr. Parker said *Triceratops* had been alive. I wondered if Cope had been a paleontologist who had conducted a dig in the Badlands back in 1892.

I glanced up at the sky. Dark, heavy clouds boiled low on the horizon. I'd have to be quick. We'd have a storm by suppertime.

I folded the maps carefully, then picked up the science journals. All but two were dated from the late 1880s. The leading article in the issue dated November 1892 was authored by Edward Drinker Cope. I scanned the article quickly.

Yes! Cope had conducted a search for dinosaurs in the Badlands. The article outlined what he had found: a few bones from a prehistoric camel and portions of a saber-toothed tiger. But no dinosaurs. Nothing from the Cretaceous period. Yet according to Cope's article, he had planned another excavation in the early summer of 1893, the very year we moved to Rim.

The journal slipped from my hand. Did Cope come to the Badlands in 1893 and what did he find? Where had he dug? Did he use Mama's maps or did she draw new ones for him?

I glanced up at the sky again. The clouds were heavier, closer. The wind was picking up, rattling the pages of the journals. I stacked them neatly in the box, along with the maps and Mama's book. I secured the box to the saddle and led Crow back down to the main track. I wouldn't have time today to visit the sites on Mama's maps. They would have to wait.

I eased Crow into a slow canter, wondering how much I should tell Mama about my plans with Dr. Parker. I wanted to use her maps, and I wanted to know if she had made others for Cope's 1893 expedition.

*Maybe you should confide in your mother.* Now Uncle Henry's words took on new meaning.

I reined Crow in as we passed through the last winding sandstone canyon before I reached my rendezvous with Stephen. I wondered again about Sally and how she had known that Mama wanted that box of papers today. And why did she have it in the first place? Maybe Mama confided in Sally Dancing Moon like I confided in Abby Hart.

In the distance, Stephen waved his hat and yelled. Lightning ripped through a yellow-green cloud, spreading fast across the sky.

*That will give you time to get used to your new name— One Who Goes Among Ghosts.*

*One who goes among Ghost* Horses? *How could she know?*

"Hurry up!" Stephen yelled over a deep rumble of thunder.

I kicked Crow into a full gallop. A violent gust of wind hit us broadside and tiny pebbles of hail bounced off my hat.

# *Chapter* II

Papa was waiting out on the porch and he waved me off Crow. I unstrapped Mama's box and hamper just as he dashed out into the street, little more than a tall dark shadow in the rain. Motioning Stephen to follow, Papa swung into the saddle and galloped down the street toward Luke's.

I shook the rain off my hat and hurried inside.

"Where's Papa going?"

Mama lit the kerosene lamp on the kitchen table. "Mrs. Brewster sent for him. She's down in her back and wanted Papa to pray with her."

"But she's a member of Reverend Cole's church."

Mama set sandwiches and potato salad on the table. "It's been like this all day. People who haven't acknowledged us in six years want to see Papa now. He's very happy." She paused, watching me wipe the mahogany box with a dishrag. "I see you got my box of papers from Sally."

I set the box on the table. "She had it ready for me when I got there."

Mama smiled and glanced out the window. The hail had stopped, but the wind blasted rain against the house.

"I'm not surprised," Mama said. "Sally always has her own way of knowing about things—especially when I send a message by her grandson." Mama's fingertips lightly brushed the top of the box. "Sit down. Papa and Stephen won't be back until late."

I poured the tea, then slipped into my place across from Mama. I helped myself to half a sandwich and potato salad, waiting for Mama to talk about her book, the science journals, the maps.

Instead she recounted everything that had happened since I had left in the morning. Who had been to see Papa and why. Mr. Knudson's fears that his store wouldn't hold the crowd when Papa preached next Sunday. And two petitions that were circulating to control what Mr. Timothy could teach in science this term—one demanding a lecture condemning Darwin's theories and one in opposition, calling for a special lecture on dinosaurs.

"Jesse Hart is circulating the dinosaur petition."

I looked up at Mama and smiled. "You mean Abby's behind it."

Mama smiled back, but her eyes were sad somehow. There was so much about her I didn't understand, so much I didn't know.

"Tell me about this," I said finally, reaching for the box and sliding it to the center of the table.

Mama opened the box slowly. She stared at its contents, her fingers curved around the edges of the lid. Her eyes filled with tears, but she didn't cry. It was as if she'd forgotten how.

"It was all so long ago," she began quietly, taking out her book. She ran her hands across the title. "I was just your age when I met Sally on a tour of the Dakotas with your grandfather." She paused and set the book aside. "These science journals are his." She handed them to me. "All I have left of his years as a publisher."

"Grandfather Stephens published this journal?" My mind raced ahead. *Then he would have known Dr. Cope. And that connection would begin to explain Mama's maps!*

Mama backed away from the table and went to the window. The rain had stopped and shafts of sunlight pierced a black wall of clouds. It was always like this in September, violent storms that swept across the plains like wildfire.

She sighed. "During your papa's sermon, I was reminded of your grandfather Stephens. And your grandmother, too. Our house in St. Louis was always simmering with new ideas. Your grandparents brought brilliant people into my life—writers, artists, scientists. I learned so much."

I wanted to ask why she gave it all up. I could only imagine living in a world like hers before Papa, a world like Uncle Henry and Aunt Eleanor's. I could never imagine giving it up, especially for a man like Papa. But the words caught in my throat.

"Tabitha, despite what your papa implied in

church, I want you to continue your study of the natural sciences." Mama turned back from the window. If she had been crying, I couldn't tell. Her eyes were clear and her voice was steady. "Maybe you'll find something interesting in your grandfather's old papers." She stopped for a moment, then smiled. "Keep them under your bed, with Uncle Henry's books—the ones you don't want Papa to find."

So Mama knew about the books Uncle Henry sent! And she had kept them a secret from Papa!

"May I keep the maps, too?" I asked, trying to keep my voice as steady as Mama's.

"The maps?"

She looked at me blankly.

"The maps of the Badlands." I pulled them out of the bottom of the box.

"Oh, those." She laughed. "Dr. Cope—what a charming man he was! I'd almost forgotten about him. One of your grandfather's friends."

Mama wiped her hands on a dish towel and returned to the table. She spread the maps out carefully, like the crocheted tablecloth we used for company.

"Dr. Cope needed maps for his excavation, but he couldn't find anyone who would come out here and map after Wounded Knee. So he asked me to draw these up, based on surveys I'd done of the Badlands before I met your father—when I was working with Sally on the book." She pointed to the sites on the map that had caught my eye that afternoon. "I cross-referenced my old survey maps against your grandfather's geological surveys of the Badlands." Her index finger rested on the word *Cretaceous*.

"But I thought Grandfather died when I was little," I said.

Mama's face clouded over. "He did, but when I was mapping for Dr. Cope, I still had most of your grandfather's papers." Her voice broke. "They were destroyed just before we moved here."

"You mean Papa destroyed them." The words were out before I could stop them.

Mama blanched. "I worked with Dr. Cope in secret, to earn the extra money we needed to make the move out here. When your papa found out, he burned your grandfather's papers, everything that belonged to my old life . . ."

"Except what you'd already sent to Sally." I finished the sentence for her.

Mama slowly folded the maps away.

" 'When I became a man, I put away childish things,' " Mama whispered, and picked up her book. "I left all this behind me when we came here. I thought it was enough to be close to Sally, to the people who told these wonderful stories." Mama opened her book to the first chapter. "But it wasn't a childish thing, Tabitha, and neither is your interest in science. I won't let your papa force you into the same mistake I made. We'll find a way. Somehow."

Mama placed her book back in the box and closed the lid.

I was ready then to tell her everything. The excavation. Dr. Parker. Tom Fortune. But there was stomping on the front porch. Papa swept inside just as I hurried into my room with Mama's box.

"I'm starved," Stephen called from the street.

I watched Mama from my room. She rearranged the sandwiches on the platter and poured out two glasses of milk.

I thought of another passage in First Corinthians. "Now we see through a glass darkly." I knew more about Mama, but I still couldn't see her clearly.

# Chapter 12

I dressed more carefully than usual for the first day of school that week, in my striped linen waist and the blue worsted skirt, the best hand-me-downs I'd ever received from the church in Kentucky. I knew girls like Kitty Olson would be watching me closely, looking for signs of repentance after Papa's sermon about me and the dinosaurs. So I planned to disappoint them: I hadn't (and wouldn't) repent anything. Besides, I wanted to look efficient and professional, like a school-teacher. After all, I'd graduate at the end of the term to teach at White River School.

I passed the post office and Abby waved me inside.

"My word, girl. Ya look like a reg'lar schoolmarm already." Abby lit a cigarette. She liked a "lighter smoke" in the morning after her first cup of coffee. "Want one?" she asked, her eyes twinkling.

"I'm on my way to school!"

"Wouldn't hurt ya none. Besides, most young fellers these days smoke sompum."

I shook by head, but I wondered if there might be

something to Abby's suggestion. Would Tom Fortune smoke a cigar? I wondered vaguely if Artie had already started smoking. I'd have to ask.

"This came fer ya bright and early." Abby produced a pale yellow Western Union envelope. "Or should I say, this came fer *Mister* Fortune." She held the telegram up to the light and squinted. "Big news, I'd say."

I snatched the envelope from her hand just as Mr. Timothy began ringing the school bell.

"Darn," I whispered under my breath. I wouldn't have time to read the telegram before school started— and I couldn't be caught reading it in public. "Darn, darn, darn," I whispered again.

"You're gonna have to learn to cuss better 'n that, girl," Abby scolded. "Not a real man this side of the Bad River would say darn at a time like this."

I slipped the telegram into my satchel.

Abby leaned over the counter. "Now *I'd* say the occasion calls for a word like—"

I shut the door before I heard her advice. Surely scholars like Uncle Henry and Dr. Parker never cursed.

Kitty Olson and a few other girls twittered when I slipped into my desk in the back row. Stephen aimed a spitball at my navy silk necktie, but it glanced off Kitty Olson's left ear and lodged in the curve of one of her elaborate braids. *Nice shot*, I thought, reaching for my *Works of Great English Literature* in the satchel.

My hand brushed against Dr. Parker's unread telegram. If it *were* addressed to Tom Fortune, like Abby said, then it had to be my official offer from Dr. Parker.

I was conscious of the telegram all morning. I could feel it, see it, lying there in the thin pocket that separated the two sections in my satchel. I had a hard time concentrating on literature and spelling. I barely listened to Mr. Timothy's short lecture on the appearance of Halley's comet in the next century. Finally the clock chimed noon.

But before I slipped outside, Mr. Timothy called me to his desk, where the course outline for a special college preparation class rested atop a stack of papers. Mr. Timothy had agreed to tutor the class for me privately since no one else was interested this term.

Mr. Timothy cleared his throat and paused. He was such a pale little man, already stoop-shouldered. He looked anxious, even nervous.

"Normally, I clear this kind of tutoring with a student's parents, something I failed to do when we originally discussed this matter. But after your father's sermon Sunday . . ." His voice trailed off.

So that was it! He was afraid of offending Papa. I said, "If you need permission, I'm sure Mama will agree."

"Good." He nodded and his thick wire-rimmed glasses bobbed up and down on his nose. "I'll discuss it with her . . . er . . . privately." He paused again.

"I've always conducted such tutorials after school. But perhaps . . ." Mr. Timothy glanced out the window. "Perhaps it would be more discreet if we worked through lunch."

"Sure." I tried to smile but turned away, disappointed in Mr. Timothy. I thought he'd have more spine.

I rushed across the street to Luke's Livery and climbed into the loft where I could read my telegram in private. I sat down behind a stack of baled hay. It smelled sweet and dry and vaguely musty. I looked at the envelope.

*Mr. Thomas Fortune*
*Rim, South Dakota*

Seeing my new name, knowing that already a man like Dr. Parker believed in it, gave me a dizzying sense of the future. My future. *This is going to happen. I am going to dig up dinosaur fossils!*

I ripped open the envelope and quickly scanned the telegram.

T. Fortune—
Salary $8 per week June–August. $36.00 advance—scouting/supplies.
Start immediately. Must thwart Harding. Wire response.
                              Dr. Phineas X. Parker

What did he mean? *Must thwart Harding*. Who was Harding, anyway? Another paleontologist?

I reread the telegram and set it aside.

Harding. *Harding*. I'd seen that name somewhere. . . . The table of contents in Uncle Henry's illustrated volume on dinosaurs? Yes, that was it. I was almost certain someone named Harding had written a chapter on dinosaur anatomy. Maybe Harding was also planning a Badlands expedition, but, if so, why would Dr. Parker care? Surely he would approve if scientific study were advanced by simultaneous expeditions.

I heard the school bell ring and slipped the telegram back in its envelope, then hid it safely in my satchel. I got to my feet and shook out my skirt. Perhaps this Harding fellow was unsound, some kind of renegade scientist. Uncle Henry had once said that not all men of science can be trusted to act honorably. It was a shocking idea—men of science who were dishonorable. It was almost more than I could believe. But maybe Harding was one of those.

The bell rang again. I hitched up my skirt and shimmied down the ladder. I had crossed the street before I realized what Dr. Parker had offered—eight dollars a week. That was more than I'd make at White River School!

I wired back right after school, accepting Dr. Parker's offer.

"Next time yer in, bring those two silver dollars

along," Abby said, pushing Jesse out of the way. She strode around the counter, the spurs on her heavy boots jingling with every step. Abby wore spurs, she said, to keep Jesse in line.

"Do you want me to start up an account then?" I asked, wondering just how far my money would go.

"Good lord, no! Don't ya know me better 'n that?" Abby shook her head, then pulled me aside. "Jesse, we need some privacy. Go on out back."

He nodded and shuffled out.

"Listen, girl," Abby said, placing her hands on my shoulders. "Yer gonna need a few things right away, things ya cain't expect ole Parker to pay fer and that ya cain't buy yer own self. Not unless ya want the whole town knowin' about it."

I remembered what Artie wrote about buying a revolver and renting a good horse.

"I do need a revolver right away," I said decisively. "And I need someone who can teach me how to use it."

"That's what I'm thinkin'." Abby reached for a half-smoked cigar smashed against the windowsill. She struck a match off the bottom of her boot. "I'll take care o' that fer ya."

"How about Saturday? We can ride out toward Cedar Pass." That was just a half mile away from one of the sites Mama's maps had identified as Cretaceous. I could kill two birds with one stone: examine formations and practice with my new revolver.

"What about yer Pa?" Abby squinted and nodded toward Knudson's.

I knew Papa was planning a Golden Girl sermon for Sunday, but with all the excitement over his dinosaur sermon, he hadn't had any time for preparation.

"I think Papa will have Golden Girls on his mind."

Abby snorted and put her hands on her hips. "Didn't know he had it in him."

# Chapter 13

I sank into Abby's old horsehair sofa, pulled off my boots, and rubbed my aching feet. My shoulders and arms throbbed from swinging a pickax. There were blisters on my hands from gripping a shovel. And those blisters had made handling my Smith & Wesson revolver harder than I'd ever imagined. My first day of practice as Tom Fortune had taught me that sheer willpower wasn't nearly enough. My body as well as my mind had to be tough to dig for dinosaur fossils— and to pass as a man in a man's world.

"If ya think ya had it bad, jist imagine if that fine Doc Parker o' yourn got hisself dressed up as a woman," Abby said, kicking shut a rickety cupboard so hard I thought it would collapse. But then, everything in the rooms Abby rented over Mr. Knudson's store looked ready to collapse.

She strode over to the table and poured out a thin amber liquid. "Fussin' with corsets and sich. A man could never make it in a woman's world." She held her glass up to the light. "Want some?"

"What is it?"

"Whiskey. Drink it for my roomatiz."

I shook my head.

"Well, maybe yer still too young." She tipped her head back and drained the glass. She rubbed her back. "Hate to say it, but I've gone soft."

I shook my head. "No you haven't." I'd had a hard time keeping up with her all day. We'd ridden twelve miles south to scout one of Grandfather Stephens's Cretaceous sites, a wide, rocky gully stretched between twin buttes—perhaps the bed of a prehistoric river.

I'd hoped for rich dinosaur deposits. But Dr. Cope had already excavated this site, and there were still traces of his work: a series of trenches worn deep over seven winters, great piles of rock, a broken wagon wheel. Abby and I had overturned rock after rock, loosened big slabs of sandstone, and dug deeper in Dr. Cope's old trenches. But we'd found nothing. And through it all, Abby kept telling me I had moved like a girl. I didn't handle the tools right, my stride was too short, my voice sounded squeaky and thin—even when I tried lowering it.

I set my boots next to the Tom Fortune clothes I'd already folded away. Abby poured one more glass of whiskey. "Leave those things where they are. I'll have Jesse warsh 'em for ya. Nothin' I hate worse 'n laundry."

"Then I can keep Tom's things here?"

"Sure thing. What else *could* ya do with 'em?

Wouldn't want yer pa to find 'em now, would we?"

She stomped back over to the cupboard, carrying her bottle of whiskey. "Where'd I put that tabbaca?"

She bent over, then growled suddenly. "If Jesse Hart weren't my own son, I'd shoot 'im. Will ya look at this!" She waved a letter in the air. "Buried under seed catalogs. *Seed catalogs*. Why, that boy wouldn't know a plow frum a gopher. Here. It's fer you. Frum Parker. Musta come today."

She handed me the letter and reached for her stash of tobacco. Before I went home, Abby had decided I should try my first cigarette. "Part a yer edication," she'd insisted.

I scanned the first two paragraphs quickly.

"What's he say?" Abby asked, before I could finish the letter. She sprinkled tobacco across a thin square of paper, then rolled it tight.

"Good news. He wants to hire you as camp cook." I read the paragraph to Abby.

Mrs. Hart's credentials look undeniably impressive. I've enclosed three of my housekeeper's most flavorful recipes, adapted for life on the trail, that Mrs. Hart should learn to master by June. They are wholesome and economical. Of course, Mrs. Hart should be prepared with her own collection of favorite camp recipes. I am not adverse to eating wild game, should it be plentiful.

"Sounds mighty finicky to me," Abby said.

I had to laugh. "You might do him some good,

Abby. Besides, he's willing to pay five dollars a week—just what you asked for."

"Ummp. We'll see. But I bet he rides sidesaddle."

I laughed again. "I thought you said men couldn't make it in a woman's world."

"Well, some of 'em act like fussy ole ladies, and I hate to say it, but this Phineas X. sounds like one who might."

Abby sealed the edge of the paper, then lit the cigarette. She reached across the table and handed it to me. "Don't suck in too fast or you'll choke."

I took the cigarette between my fingers and watched a thin ring of ash form around the end. Couldn't this experiment wait until next time? Still, I had to be convincing. Closing my eyes, I placed the cigarette between my lips. The tobacco smell was rich, almost pleasant. Maybe this wouldn't be too bad. I inhaled lightly. A big, smoky glob lodged in the back of my throat and moved up my nasal passages. I spit it back out, coughing and gagging.

"Give it time, girl. By June you'll be smokin' like a cowpuncher." She reached into her pocket for a cigar. "Though I hear tell some mighty fine and edicated ladies back East are takin' to it now." She paused. "Come to think of it, maybe ya should take up chewin'. Not so girlie, if ya know what I mean."

I coughed again and looked back down at Dr. Parker's letter.

"What else does he say?" Abby settled back in her chair and blew smoke rings at the ceiling.

Cigarette smoke curled up my nose and stung my
eyes. This was harder than handling a six-shooter with
blisters on your hands. I squinted and read the next
paragraph out loud.

I am not opposed to using Dr. Cope's old maps as
a reference. Nor would I prohibit one of his virgin
sites. But under no circumstances will I begin
work at a site where he failed. Dinosaurs rather
than extinct mammals are our objective.

"What's he mean by that?" Abby asked, tipping her
chair back, legs propped up on the table.

I put the cigarette to my lips and inhaled again. My
head was beginning to ache.

"Speak up, girl."

I sputtered and gasped for breath. "It means," I
said, coughing, "he doesn't want to dig where we were
today—or anyplace else where Dr. Cope has been." I
snuffed out the cigarette and went to the open window. The air felt cool, fresh.

"Could be good. Could be bad. Depends on what ya
find out there." Abby joined me by the window. She
slapped me on the back. "Ain't sick, are ya?"

I shook my head and breathed in great gulps of air.
My mind cleared and I thought about Dr. Parker's
instructions. Grandfather Stephens's Cretaceous sites
on Mama's maps were my best and only leads. There
were five more sites. How many of those had Cope
already excavated? How many would have dinosaur

bones? Right now there was no way to know. I'd just have to scout every site and hope for the best. But time was running out.

"I've got to find an excavation site before I leave for White River in January," I said slowly. "It may be harder than I thought."

"Don't worry, Tom. You'll see yer way through. Here." She reached for an old bottle labeled *Eau des Violettes*. "Take a swig a this afore ya go home. It'll kill the smell a tabbaca."

I slipped back home while Papa was locked away in his study, preparing for the next day's sermon.

"What were you doing with Abby all day?" Mama asked. She pushed a piece of apple pie across the table. I folded my hands in my lap, hoping she wouldn't notice the blisters.

"A science project on fossils. Abby volunteered to help." It wasn't a brilliant excuse, but maybe it would work.

"I didn't realize Abby was so interested in fossils." Mama turned away and carried another piece of pie in to Papa.

I slipped into my room and shut the door, pulling Dr. Parker's letter out of my pocket. The second and third pages were about the mysterious Dr. Harding and his unprofessional conduct at a dig in Montana. It was hard to follow. But one paragraph was perfectly clear.

It has been confirmed by one of my own trusted assistants that Harding plans a full-scale excavation in the Badlands during June and July, no doubt a feeble attempt to thwart my own plans. A.V. Harding is a scandalous, publicity-seeking scientist, though I hesitate to apply the word to one such as Harding. Be careful not to reveal our plans to those in Harding's employ, no matter how seemingly harmless they may appear. Harding's staff is a treacherous lot. If, however, you glean any information about their plans from your own sources, contact me immediately.

> Sincerely,
> Phineas X. Parker, Ph.D.

Despite Dr. Parker's warning, I still couldn't help feeling that it might be better to cooperate with Dr. Harding's staff. Surely cooperation rather than secrecy would further the ends of scientific discovery. I decided to write Uncle Henry for advice. Perhaps he knew Harding or why Dr. Parker felt he was so threatening.

My eyes dropped to the postscript, a long quotation from a new book Dr. Parker said he was reading. I read the paragraph again and again.

"Without a doubt there exist some distinguished women, very superior to the average man, but they are as exceptional as the birth of any monstrosity as, for example, of a gorilla with two heads; consequently, we may neglect them entirely."

Dr. Parker had underlined "a gorilla with two heads." Did he already suspect me?

There was a soft knock on my bedroom door.

I stuffed Dr. Parker's letter under my pillow. "Come in," I called, reaching for my Bible and pretending to read.

Mama pushed the door open lightly and handed me a jar of ointment. "For your blisters," she whispered. "And remember to wear your gloves to church in the morning."

## Chapter 14

I tightened my belt and straightened my trousers, then moved around to the other side of Abby's buckboard. I took long strides, feeling the heels of my boots dig into the ground when I walked. I reached for my jacket and hat. The November sky was clear. Sunshine glittered off a nearby stock pond. But the air was tangy and cool. This might be our last Badlands trip until spring.

"Ya don't look half bad, Tom," Abby called from the boulder where she was arranging tin cans. She wore a heavy serge skirt tucked up at the waist, revealing a pair of buckskin pants underneath. "Lookin' better every week!" She spit a wad of tobacco and it arched over the boulder like a dingy rainbow.

I reached for my Smith & Wesson revolver and smiled.

Abby was right. Two months of practice as Tom Fortune was beginning to pay off. I walked more like Artie, my weight balanced over a wider stance, a longer stride. My hands were calloused, not blistered. I swung a pickax like a man.

I opened the revolver's cylinder, counted out six bullets, and slipped them in. My fingers moved easily, almost as skillfully as Abby's.

"Ready?" she called.

I nodded and looked up at her, twelve feet away. She stepped aside and reached into her pocket for another chew, pretending not to watch me closely. But I could feel her eyes on me, measuring my every move.

I cocked the Smith & Wesson, then shot quickly, barely stopping to aim.

*Ping. Ping. Ping. Ping.*

Four of the six cans flew off the boulder and rolled down toward Crow. He flicked his tail and snorted.

"Not bad, but I've seen ya do better."

I slid my six-shooter back in its holster as Abby picked up the cans. Despite her weak praise, I *was* getting better. In the beginning, she had me aim slowly, carefully. Now she had me working faster.

"A rattlesnake ain't gonna wait fer ya to aim afore he strikes," she had said in October. "Ya gotta learn to shoot quick. Shoot straight."

Abby lined the cans up again, then reached for the canteen she wore slung over her shoulder. She looked up at the sky, a clear, frosty blue.

"Makes me think of them old days with Calamity." She tilted her head back and drank long and loud, then wiped her mouth on the back of her hand. "Good days they were. Nothing like the company of a strong woman." She paused. "Kinda hate to think about putting up with a passel o' men come spring."

Dr. Parker's last letter had announced that in addition to his fossil preparator, three student assistants—male assistants, we assumed—would be coming out, too. Abby wasn't pleased. "Jist more mouths to feed," she'd said.

But I was much more worried about finding the right place to dig. There was just one Cretaceous site on Mama's map left to explore. Abby and I had scouted the others in September and October. We found signs of Dr. Cope's work at all five. But despite Dr. Parker's order not to dig where Dr. Cope had failed, I looked for dinosaur fossils anyway. The work was long and hard, but never tedious—even though I didn't find anything. I learned to love the rhythm of the pickax, the suspense of turning over a slab of sandstone.

I reloaded my six-shooter and nodded at Abby. She moved down toward Crow and motioned for me to shoot.

I fired another round.

*Ping. Ping. Ping. Ping. Ping. Ping.*

"Like that any better?" I called, pleased with my performance. I reloaded as Abby collected the cans.

"Let's try sompum new," she called down between chews. "Ya shoot when I throw. Jist be careful ya don't shoot *me*—or Crow here."

*Ping. Ping. Ping. Ping. Ping.*

Five out of six.

Abby spit a wad of tobacco. "Ya take to this real nat'ral. Never seen anything like it afore." Her praise was rare, precious. "Yer a credit to yer sex, girl." She winked. "Whatever ya are, that is."

I laughed and motioned Abby over to the buckboard. "Let me show you where I'm going today."

Abby cocked an eyebrow. This was our sixth Badlands trip, but I'd never gone off on my own.

I spread Mama's map out over the seat and pointed to a spot three miles away. It was the last Cretaceous site, the farthest from home.

"I don't think your buckboard will make it," I said. "The country's too rugged."

Abby shaded her eyes and looked over a wall of jagged Badlands spires.

"Think yer right, Tom. The pass through them hills is too steep and narrow. How long do ya think you'll be?"

I folded the map away. "A couple of hours. It's an easy ride until I get to the ridge."

I swung into the saddle and wrapped a canteen around the saddle horn. I slid my Smith & Wesson into its holster.

"Fire three times if there's trouble. I ken ride this ole cart horse bareback if I have to." Abby sent one long blob of spit under her horse's nose. "I'll be waitin' fer ya."

I waved good-bye and spurred Crow into a slow canter. I could make good time for the first two miles; the last one was more risky.

My long braid bounced against my back and I thought about the question Abby had asked me that morning.

"How do ya feel about this?" Abby had crinkled up her eyes and tugged at my braid, which hung halfway to my waist. "Could you part with all this hair?"

It wouldn't be an impossible sacrifice, although my hair was my best feature. Thick and black and wavy, like Papa's. But if it ever spilled out of my hat, Dr. Parker would fire me on the spot. *A gorilla with two heads*. Why had he written that? I couldn't help feeling he had begun to doubt me.

But the more I thought about it, the angrier I became. I wasn't a monster. Neither was Mama. Or Abby. Or Sally Dancing Moon. A chilling voice inside my head whispered, "He sounds like Papa; he sounds like Papa."

I pushed the thought away. No one could be as unreasonable as Papa.

I passed a noisy prairie-dog town and slowed Crow to a walk. We were moving up the first ridge of narrow hills and the trail was rocky and steep. I'd probably have to get off and lead Crow down the other side. At least I wasn't in a hurry today.

It had been easy to slip away from Papa. It always was now. His sermons had become extremely popular, and people from as far away as Rapid City drove out to hear him. They came into town on Saturday night—by train or wagon—stayed overnight, then left Sunday right after church. In fact, the whole town was booming. Mr. Knudson was taking in boarders. Sister Porter even cooked Saturday-night fried-chicken suppers, which out-of-towners ate because they didn't know any better.

But Papa had moved beyond dinosaurs and Golden Girls. His new sermons were all about the "evils of the modern age": *Unholy Freedoms for the Weaker Sex*; *The Hidden Dangers of Electrical Devices*; *Wanton Pleasures of the New Century*. But these new sermons needed research—or at least, Papa's version of research. He pored over the outdated newspapers and magazines that came to us from the church in Kentucky. He even subscribed to *The Rapid City Journal*.

"I need to know the evil forces at work in the modern world," he said.

So, on Saturdays, he shut himself in his study with his "modern sources of potential evil" and didn't notice that I wasn't home till dark.

And Mama didn't ask any questions.

I reached the summit of the first ridge, and the trail zigzagged almost straight down to the bottom of a narrow canyon. It looked like rattlesnake country. Rattlers were aggressive and angry on days like this, looking for their winter dens. I swung my leg over Crow, eased out of the saddle, and drew out my six-shooter. With my Smith & Wesson in one hand and Crow's lead in the other, I inched down the trail. Crow picked his way down steadily, gingerly. Loose pebbles skittered under my boots and I slipped twice. But we reached the canyon floor safely.

I mounted Crow again and headed up the last sandstone ridge. It was a long climb, twisting and narrow, but smooth. At the top the trail broke away suddenly and opened to a wide box canyon, Grandfather Stephens's final Cretaceous site. I glanced down and realized that the trail turned off abruptly to the right, then gently snaked to the bottom of the canyon—an easy ride. I was on the canyon floor in minutes.

The walls of the canyon were pebbly and glittery, jutting high against the sky at the north end, stunted but smooth at the south. Unlike the other sites, there were no signs of previous digging: no trenches, no camp debris, no discarded tools. Obviously Dr. Cope and his party hadn't reached this canyon in 1892 or '93, and that's what Dr. Parker wanted.

The rock here was layered in distinct colors. Brown, red, pink, yellow. I ran my fingers over the rock and traced the pattern. I wished I knew more about geology.

I unstrapped my shovel and pickax from the saddle and glanced around the canyon. Where to begin? The sun glinted off a jagged ledge of sandstone about twenty feet up against the north wall. There was something curious about it, a piece of exposed rock that didn't match the sediment colors around it.

I dropped my tools and ran toward the ledge. A narrow cut, barely wide enough for one person, sliced the canyon wall and snaked up, up to the ledge. I scrambled up on all fours and knelt by what had to be bone. My hands trembled as I ran my fingers across its surface. Prehistoric bone. A rough edge on smooth stone.

I bent to look closer.

A thick, jagged piece of fossilized bone, perhaps four inches long, jutted out of the ledge. I closed my eyes, trying to remember what little I knew of lizard anatomy. I *knew* this yellowed piece of bone belonged to a dinosaur. I had no proof, only instinct.

I glanced down around the canyon, imagining a different world. A muddy river with dense, green trees clustered around its banks. The smell of fear in the air. Had this animal met its death here—swept away by a sudden flood or torn to pieces by some great carnivore?

I touched the fossil again, and my hands stopped shaking.

I spent the next hour investigating the rest of the canyon, but I found nothing more than that first piece of bone. Was it an isolated fossil or could the rest of the animal be buried beneath the sandstone ledge?

On the back side of Mama's map, I sketched what I could see of the bone. I'd recopy it later and send it along with a description of the find to Dr. Parker on Monday. Then I pulled out my pocket watch. Two o'clock. I needed to get back to Abby. It would be dark by five-thirty.

I glanced around the canyon, making quick mental notes, then mounted Crow. Mama's map seemed accurate. If we dug here next June, the main camp would have to be back where Abby was waiting by the stock pond. It would be virtually impossible to haul water and pack supplies into this canyon. But if we found something really big, if that jutting piece of bone were part of a massive carnivore, how would we get it out? A complete dinosaur skeleton could weigh hundreds of pounds. Was that why Dr. Cope and his party had chosen to dig elsewhere? Maybe there was another way in and out of the canyon. I'd have to come back.

My progress back to Abby was slow and tedious. Afternoon shadows now deepened every snaky crevice. Even Crow seemed jumpy. But I reminded myself that any snakes would be out in the sun, not hiding in the chilly afternoon shade.

I was right.

At the crest of the last hill, six maybe seven feet below the trail, a big rattler stretched out in the sun. But it let us pass without a single rattle and Crow, smart horse that he was, didn't spook.

# Chapter 15

It was cold, so very cold. Winter had settled in during the last two weeks. I huddled down deeper in the saddle and glanced up at the sky. It had been clear when I left. Now a low bank of gray clouds hovered in the west. There would be snow later, maybe the season's first blizzard. I spurred Crow into a gallop and his hooves thudded on the frozen Badlands floor.

I was following an old wagon trace that skirted what I now called Ghost Horse Canyon. The trace came within a quarter mile of the canyon's southern edge, where the formations that walled off the canyon were low and shallow. Maybe, just maybe, we could build a ramp there, a ramp sturdy enough to support a wagon—and a dinosaur.

The sky grew darker, lower, closer. The supplies I'd packed for Sally Dancing Moon—my excuse for being out in the Badlands alone—thumped against the saddle. For a moment I wondered if I should turn back. But I was so close, and I might not get a chance like this again until spring.

I tethered Crow and walked toward the short, sloping formation that marked the canyon's lowest and most accessible point. Up close, it looked like a golden-pink dollop of mashed potatoes. I could just see over the top, into the canyon itself.

I found a foothold along the rounded wall and pushed myself up. My boot slipped and I slid down, landing on my back. Slowly I got to my feet, feeling thick and sluggish, wrapped in too many clothes. I tried again, and this time I was up.

The rock wall was about five feet high, perhaps eight feet long, and just wide enough for a buckboard and mules. The ground below was relatively smooth—only a few ruts. Yes, this would work. I peeled off my gloves, pulled out my notebook, and made a clumsy sketch of the formations, an even clumsier one of the ramp. Then a blast of wind cut through all my heavy clothes and sent my gloves flying across the canyon. I had to go.


Sally's cabin huddled against the pines, as gray and dark as the snow clouds churning in the west. Her tipi was gone, and Sally was gone, too. Where had she seen the ghost horses she used to tell me about? My question would have to wait until spring.

I mounted Crow and we raced back toward home, the blizzard a silver ghost whispering ice in my ears. Still there was no snow. But by the time I reached the last Badlands formation before town, Rim was nothing

more than a gray shadow shivering against the sky.
Wind whipped against my face. Snow caught in my
eyelashes. There wasn't time to collect the skirt I'd left
in the sandstone crevice that morning. I'd have to go
home in my Tom Fortune costume and take my
chances with Papa.

Mama and Abby were waiting for me on the porch.

"Thank God," Mama said, hugging me close.

"Good ta see ya, Tabbie." Abby took Crow's reins
as an explosion of wind and snow hit the side of the
house. "I'll let the menfolk know she's back, Miz Fortune." Abby turned toward Luke's.

Mama drew me inside. If she noticed my clothes,
she didn't say anything.

"We just got word about an hour ago that Sally's
already moved to Pine Ridge for the winter." She
paused and laid her hand against my cheek. "Your
papa doesn't want you traveling alone out there, and
he's probably right. It's too dangerous."

I peeled off layers of wool while Mama poured me a
cup of tea.

"Where is Papa?" I asked finally.

"He's at Luke's, organizing your search party."

# *Chapter 16*

I put my pencil down and folded my hands in my lap. Mr. Timothy and the state teachers examiners, two men still bundled in greatcoats, stood at the front of the school, under the ticking Regulator clock. There were still twenty minutes to wait before I could turn in my examination, but I was already finished and had double-checked my answers. The test had been easier than I thought it would be.

Mr. Timothy walked up the aisle and stopped by my desk. "Have you completed your examination?" he whispered.

I nodded.

"The examiners will take your test now. They'll grade it while they're waiting for the others to finish."

"Fine," I said, reaching for the coat and hat I'd laid across the next desk. I nodded good-bye to the examiners and shook hands with Mr. Timothy.

Then I was outside.

The wind hit me hard, making my eyes sting, sucking out my breath. A low wall of heavy clouds clung to the western horizon like clumps of oatmeal. The examiners would never make it back to Pierre in time for Christmas the next day.

I hurried home, not even stopping to see Abby. The cold was too fierce. If this kept up, I might not make it out to White River. Mr. Gilfillan was coming for me the day after Christmas, so I could open the school right after New Year's.

The wind caught our front door and I burst into the kitchen on a cold blast of air. Mama looked up, startled. She sat on the floor surrounded by three big shipping boxes.

"I was afraid you might be Papa." She looked worried. "These arrived from Uncle Henry and Aunt Eleanor while you were out."

The fire in the stove popped and crackled, pushing back the cold pressing in against the walls. I tugged off my coat and sank to the floor. We'd never received so much from them before!

I remembered Papa's parting words to Uncle Henry in September: "We won't be back again." There was no way Papa would let us keep all this, and there was no way he wouldn't notice it.

The box Mama had opened was filled with clothing and books. Mountains of books.

"Uncle Henry seems more generous than usual this year," Mama said, arching an eyebrow and handing me a stack of heavy, dull-colored texts. "Most of them seem to be about dinosaurs." Her eyes narrowed.

"Where are Papa and Stephen?" I asked, changing the subject.

Mama turned away and pulled out a beautiful paisley shawl. She held it up to the light.

"They're with Sister Porter. She had a mild heart seizure this morning."

These days Papa insisted that Stephen follow him everywhere. Odd how I had so much freedom now and Stephen had so little. Maybe Papa had decided that Stephen had sown enough wild oats.

I opened a heavy brown volume entitled *Collected Essays on the Prehistoric World* and turned to the table of contents, hoping that perhaps Dr. Parker or the mysterious Dr. Harding might be listed as contributors.

"Tabitha, what do you make of this?" Mama asked, holding up a pair of what had to be Artie's old trousers. "They're far too long for Stephen. And there's more." Mama eyed me suspiciously. "Two shirts, another pair of trousers, suspenders, a vest . . ."

I scrambled to my feet and grabbed Artie's things from Mama's hands. Without thinking, I said, "They're—ah—they're for a boy at White River School. I asked Artie if he could spare any castoffs—and I'm so glad he could."

I hurried into my room before Mama could ask more questions and folded Artie's clothes under a layer of petticoats in Mama's open steamer trunk. I had packed most of my things for White River the day before, leaving room on top for the books I expected from Uncle Henry.

I didn't hear Papa and Stephen until they were already in the kitchen. I watched from the doorway, my heart aching for the stacks of unprotected books heaped around the stove.

"What is all this?" Papa thundered, reaching for the paisley shawl Mama had draped over a kitchen chair.

Stephen dropped to the floor and ripped open the second box. It was filled with beautifully wrapped Christmas packages.

"I thought I told you we would *never* have any more contact with your sister and brother-in-law! Their worldliness is an abomination."

Papa's voice was cold, hard, mean. I'd never seen him talk to Mama like that.

He threw the shawl on the floor and kicked the box of Christmas packages out of Stephen's reach. "We will *not* live on their charity."

Mama picked up the shawl and folded it across her arms. "We're not living off their charity," she blazed back, her eyes flashing. "These are *Christmas* presents."

I'd never heard Mama talk back to Papa like that— and never in front of Stephen and me.

"The ill-gotten gains of science should never touch a family in the service of the Almighty." Papa snatched the shawl from Mama.

It ripped down the middle.

The color drained from Mama's face. "I don't care how your foolish pride affects me," she whispered, gathering up what was left of the shawl. "But think of all you're denying our children!" Her glance fell on me, then shifted to the box of books on the floor.

Papa followed her gaze.

Slowly, slowly, he knelt to read the titles.

One by one, he lifted a book, then set it aside.

Finally he turned to Mama and hissed, "So this is what I'm denying my children. The misguided, nay, *unholy* universe of scientific thought." His voice rose. " 'What does it profit a man if he gain the whole world and lose his own soul.' What kind of mother are you to risk your child's immortal soul! Well, I won't let you!"

Then he turned on me.

Papa grabbed my arm in one hand, a box of books in the other, and dragged me over to the stove. "See how fast the fire burns."

He forced me to my knees and opened the stove door, sending a wave of heat across my face. Papa threw a book into the flames. "Be glad this is just a book and not your soul."

He reached for another. I struggled to stop him, but he was too strong. Two books, three books went into the fire. It singed my hair, my eyes stung. But that didn't matter. Papa was burning my future.

I struggled harder, but Papa's hold on me tightened, sucking out all my breath. I tried to scream, but nothing came out. I reached for one book, then another. But they were always just beyond my grasp, lingering before my eyes an instant before Papa pitched them into the stove.

The flames flickered and spewed black smoke. My

throat stung and my eyes watered. But I wasn't crying. Not yet. Not in front of Papa. I clawed his arm. My fingernails dug into his wrist.

"That's enough, Charles!" Mama tried to wrench me away. "*That's enough!*" She reached for the last three books in the bottom of the box, but Papa was faster. He scooped them up, then pushed the box away, shoving Mama back across the table.

Suddenly the front door burst open and there was Mr. Timothy and the two teachers examiners, standing in a swirl of snow. Papa threw the last three books into the fire, then closed the stove.

I fell back on the floor, weak from anger, my arm throbbing from Papa's grasp.

Mr. Timothy cleared his throat. "I apologize for catching you at an inopportune moment, Reverend Fortune, Mrs. Fortune. We knocked but no one answered."

Papa and Mama were silent. Stephen eased around the corner into Papa's study. I stumbled to my feet.

Finally Papa said in his best preacher voice, "Why are you here, gentlemen?"

Mr. Timothy took off his hat and squinted through his frosty glasses. "It's about Tabitha, sir. She's done something rather remarkable." He fingered his thin mustache, something he always did when he was nervous. His hand shook. "She's scored the highest marks ever on the State Teachers Examination. One hundred percent."

The short, burly examiner handed me a square piece

of parchment. It was my teaching certificate. He shook my hand heartily. "A pleasure to have met you, Miss Fortune." He turned to Papa. "You should be very proud of your daughter, Reverend Fortune. She has a bright and promising career ahead of her."

Then they were gone. I wished I could go with them.

I spent Christmas Day locked in my room. It was part of my punishment, but for once I agreed with Papa's action. I had no desire to hear his Christmas sermon. And I had no desire to help Stephen distribute our Christmas presents from Uncle Henry and Aunt Eleanor to needy families in town. Neither did Mama.

Papa and Stephen ate Christmas dinner at the Porters'.

Mama and I had cold corn bread and weak tea.


Mr. Gilfillan arrived early the next morning. He helped me into his sleigh, and I turned to wave good-bye to Mama and Stephen. Papa had left before dawn to pray with Sister Porter. I was glad he wasn't home when I left.

The horses pranced up the street, their bells jingling in the clear, frosty sunshine.

Abby hailed us from the post office and Mr. Gilfillan reined in his pair of matched bays.

"Jesse plum' forgot this here package fer ya, Tabbie. Came with the others Christmas Eve. It's frum yer uncle back in Mitchell." She handed me a small but heavy box, then patted my shoulder. Abby didn't believe in kissing and hugging.

"Take kere a yisself, girl. See ya come spring."

Mr. Gilfillan clucked to the horses and the town quickly gave way to a flat, open plain of dazzling white nothingness.

Just before sunset, I unwrapped Uncle Henry's package in my tiny lean-to room off the Gilfillans' kitchen. It was a book, one large volume: *Vertebrata of the Tertiary Formations of the West* by Edward Drinker Cope.

I smiled and hugged it to my chest. Never again would I complain about Postmaster Jesse Hart's untimely deliveries.

# *Chapter 17*

## (Five Months Later)

I closed the whitewashed door behind me and slipped the key into my pocket. The children raced across the short grass, book straps slung across their shoulders. Lawrence. Maddie. Wilma. Trudy. Hattie. And Emit.

Trudy turned and yelled, "Good-bye, Miss Fortune. See you next fall!"

I waved, then shaded my eyes. Out on the horizon, silhouetted against a soft spring sky, was a slow-moving buckboard. I squinted, hoping Stephen was the driver, knowing in my heart that it was Papa coming to take me back.

I crossed the schoolyard to the house where Mrs. Gilfillan was waiting at the door. She held out a pale blue envelope with my name on it.

"The school board wants you back in the fall, Tabitha," she said, as I took the envelope. "You've been the best teacher my little ones have ever had." She paused and looked out at Papa's wagon, edging ever closer. "I hope you'll board with us again. You're a real good girl."

I followed her gaze across the prairie. Papa would be here in just a few minutes, and with him would come the end of the freedom I'd learned to cherish at White River. I liked being my own person, making my own rules. Then I reminded myself that soon I'd have even more freedom. Tom Fortune could do all the things that I'd always dreamed about. If all went according to plan, in just a few days I'd be out on my own, searching for ghost horses.

I walked through Mrs. Gilfillan's spotless kitchen to my room. I shut the door and slowly opened the letter from the school board. It offered me White River School for the entire academic year of 1900/1901—*plus* a fifteen percent increase in salary. There was also a ten-dollar bonus for "Outstanding Performance during the Spring Term of 1900." I appreciated their generosity, yet I hoped I wouldn't have to return in September. Surely my entire world would be different after a summer as Tom Fortune in the Badlands. I had a vague hope that somehow Dr. Parker would accept me as *Tabitha* Fortune and encourage me to study with him at Yale.

"Tabitha," Mrs. Gilfillan called, "your pa's here to fetch you home."

I glanced around the room one more time, then pinned on my shapeless straw hat. Papa hadn't written me once since I'd been gone. What would we say to each other? I hadn't missed him and I doubted that he'd missed me. I opened the door.

Papa stood in the doorway, tall in his dusty second-best suit.

"Let's go, Tabitha Ruth," he said, without smiling. "We have things to talk about."

I was glad he didn't hug me.

I said good-bye to Mrs. Gilfillan, who wrapped me in her sturdy arms and kissed me soundly on the forehead. "Come back to us in September," she whispered.

Emit and Papa loaded Mama's trunk. It thudded against the wagon bed, causing the whole buckboard to heave.

"Seems heavier than when you left home," Papa noted.

I didn't say anything because my trunk *was* heavier, much heavier—and not just from Professor Cope's book. When Uncle Henry heard that Papa had destroyed all my books, he sent a second copy of the three most important texts, including a massive one on reptile anatomy. Jesse had delivered them to White River himself. In fact, Abby had Jesse making regular mail runs to White River so I didn't miss a single letter from Dr. Parker all winter—and Mama got my monthly teaching checks regularly.

I climbed into the wagon seat. A copy of *The Rapid City Journal* lay under Papa's big black hat. The edges of the paper rustled in the breeze like dry corn shucks.

"Read this, Tabitha," Papa said, handing me the

paper. His hands shook ever so slightly. "Then tell me what you think of your father now." He clucked at the horses and we lurched ahead.

"Dynamic Voice in the Wilderness Cries Out to a Degenerate Age," the headline read. Underneath it was a picture of Papa, looking stern and fierce in his best Sunday suit, his big battered Bible tucked under his right arm. I glanced at the dateline.

April 15, 1900.

That was weeks ago. Why hadn't Mama written me about it?

I scanned the article quickly. It talked about Papa's sermons on the "evils of the coming twentieth century: women's suffrage and emancipation, the machine age, evolution, lewd and permissive behavior." The article concluded:

> *Clearly, the Reverend Charles Fortune is a Beacon in the Wilderness, a Light on the Hill. His sermons remind us that Change is not always Progress. Crowds flock to his Sunday sermons in a humble storefront on the edge of the Badlands. They like to say, "The Reverend Fortune is a much-needed Voice, crying out in the Wilderness." Surely, however, he need not confine his ministry to the Wilderness. Let us pray that he can find the Will to bring his Ministry to our Fair City, which sorely needs the wisdom of such a Man in these Dangerous Times.*

In the very last paragraph, the reporter mentioned that Papa was an upstanding family man, the father of two "wholesome" children, Tabitha Ruth and Stephen James. Mama wasn't even mentioned.

I folded the paper back up and set it between us on the seat.

A pronghorn and her twins skittered across the wagon track. Cloud shadows raced across the prairie toward the horizon.

"Have you nothing to say, Tabitha?" Papa asked finally.

I thought he sounded disappointed, but what could I say? These *were* dangerous times if even a big-city reporter believed intolerance passed for enlightenment.

"I thought as much." He cleared his throat. "Your mama felt that the time at White River would free your mind and spirit. But I see now it's only hardened your heart against me."

Papa didn't wait for me to respond.

"I have planned to take your mama and Stephen with me back to the church in Kentucky. We will embark on our journey next week," he said, looking straight ahead.

*"Your mama and Stephen!" Did that mean he didn't want to take me? That would make everything so much easier!*

"What's the purpose of this trip?" I asked, trying to keep my voice steady.

"We will spend a few days in Hot Springs while I research sermons on divorce and the indulgence of earthly pleasures."

I looked away. Papa had long forbidden an excursion to Hot Springs because he always felt it was a den of iniquity, a city where people of loose morals ended their marriages and sought physical pleasure in public bathing.

"Then on to Kentucky," he explained. "I will ask the church for a reassignment to Rapid City and funds to establish a new church there. Clearly, I have had a calling to a new mission."

Without thinking I asked, "How does Mama feel about this?"

He looked at me as if I had spoken in tongues. "Have your months away from home wiped the slate on your heart clean? 'For the husband is the head of the wife, even as Christ is the head of the church.' Your mother will follow me."

I thought about the trips Mama took into the Badlands, nursing sick children, teaching entire families how to read. Somehow that seemed more meaningful than preaching flashy sermons in a big-city church.

"Do the elders in Kentucky know anything about your plans?" I asked.

"I've sent them the newspaper clipping," Papa said, "but I want to discuss the matter with them personally. They need to hear me speak. See me with my family."

"But you want me to stay behind." I had to know why Papa didn't want me in Kentucky.

We topped a shallow hill and Rim lay below us in the distance.

Papa reined in the horses. "The elders will be interested in the authority I now command in the region and at home. You're obviously a successful school-teacher now, a testimony to the fine upbringing you've had in our home." Papa's voice almost quivered. "But your presence isn't necessary—unlike Stephen, who is still a child, a young servant of God at an impression-able age."

Was Papa afraid I'd ruin his chance of getting a new church? Was he ready to give me my freedom? It was an exhilarating idea, like watching a purple-green twister rip up the sod way out on the horizon from the safety of your cellar door.

"We should be back home in Rim by the end of July," Papa continued. "In the meantime, your mother has arranged for Mrs. Hart to look in on you while we're gone." He said *Mrs. Hart* as if her name itself were poison.

"*Abby?*" I said.

"I suggested Sister Porter," he said stiffly, "but your mother insisted on Mrs. Hart. She reminded me that you and Sister Porter have never been close."

I looked down at the newspaper again. Had Mama agreed to go to Kentucky with Papa only if I stayed behind with Abby? I glanced over at Papa. His face looked sad but determined. *He must want this church with all his heart*, I realized suddenly. *No matter what the price. . . .*

Papa clucked to the horses again and we moved down the last hill toward Rim. The town looked clean and fresh in the distance, like a brilliant morning glory just waiting to be picked.

"We leave June sixth."

*June sixth!* I couldn't help smiling. All the elaborate arrangements, the plans I'd laid to slip away from Papa—now I wouldn't need them. I was about to become Tom Fortune without any of the roadblocks I'd imagined.

# Chapter 18

"Thanks for the homecoming yesterday," I said, as the post office door slapped shut behind me.

"Twarn't nothin'," said Abby, blowing a perfectly shaped smoke ring toward the back room. "Anybody could a done it."

"That's not true, Abby, and you know it." Actually, the whole town had gotten behind Abby's idea. There was a WELCOME HOME, TABITHA banner, a speech from Mr. Timothy, lemonade and strawberry pie—and Luke had even given me Crow to ride for the whole summer, no charge.

"Jist b'tween us, I'm mighty sorry about ole Knudson's tuba." Abby's spurs jingled as she walked around the counter. "He sure ain't no John Philip Sousa." Mr. Knudson's rendition of "He's a Jolly Good Fellow" had spooked the horses over at Luke's and sent everybody home early.

"Well, as Papa always says, he shouldn't have gone to so much trouble."

Abby snorted. She thrust a stack of envelopes in my direction. "Fer you."

There were two from Dr. Parker, one from Uncle Henry, and three fat, oversized envelopes with elaborate printing on the outside. They were from the school boards in Pierre, Mitchell, and Rapid City.

"Offers from all three," Abby noted. "I steamed 'em open when they come in. Didn't think ya'd mind." She chewed on the end of her cigar and shook her head. "Best one's from Mitchell. Pity, though, if after all this trouble ya become a schoolmarm."

Abby was right. Teaching had given me an escape from Papa and the chance to study the subjects I needed to know before the expedition—reptile anatomy, recent dinosaur discoveries, fossil preservation techniques—but I couldn't really see myself as a schoolteacher.

I looked out at Main Street. Mama emerged from Knudson's store with Stephen behind her, carrying a basket heaping with supplies—flour, sugar, bolts of gingham. Mama looked tired, her lips drawn in a tight, narrow line. Abby joined me at the window.

"Your ma's had a real tough winter. Mighty fine woman, though."

There was suddenly a lump in my throat, big and hard and impossible to swallow. How tight and close she'd held me yesterday when I jumped out of the wagon.

"I guess she missed me more than I knew."

Abby crushed out her cigar and snorted again. "Don't blame yerself, girl. It's that pa a yourn, I reckon. How she's lived with that man all these years is a tribute to the patience a womanhood."

I turned and waited for Abby to continue, suddenly remembering the violence in Papa's voice on Christmas Eve, the way Mama had defied him.

"Still," Abby said finally, "I'll say this fer your pa." She paused and lit a fresh cigar. "He let me give that party fer ya yesterday. Didn't think he would. 'Everyone needs their moment a glory,' he said."

I wondered if Papa had ever given Mama her moment of glory. I nodded good-bye and opened the door.

"Say," Abby called out. "Forgot to mention, the advance man for that Harding crew will be out on Sunday. Comin' in on the eleven-forty-five from Pierre. 'Spect that's what them letters from Parker is about."

On Sunday at least sixty people crammed into Knudson's store. More spilled out onto the front porch and into the street. I'd never seen so many people in town before—all to hear Papa preach his last sermon before leaving for Hot Springs and the church in Kentucky. Mama, Stephen, and I had given up our seats to a family from Rapid City.

" 'This know also,' " Papa quoted, " 'that in the last

days perilous times shall come.' Those perilous times are here and now. A new century is dawning and with it an age that loves pleasure more than God."

I had to admit that Papa could be an entertaining—if unenlightened—speaker, something I'd forgotten while I was away. Still, I couldn't miss Dr. Harding's advance man. I clicked open the watch pinned on the lapel of my white linen suit. Eleven-thirty. I eased my way slowly back to the door and slipped behind Buck Lowry. I opened my Bible and unfolded one of Dr. Parker's most recent letters.

"Harding is a careless and unscrupulous researcher," he had written. "Yet you must keep me informed of *every* development. I must know where Harding plans to dig. But I charge you, Thomas, to shroud the plans for our own operation in secrecy. *Do not*, under any circumstances, reveal our fossil site to Harding or Harding's assistants. *Do not* be misled by *charm*."

Papa's voice rose and fell dramatically. I folded Dr. Parker's letter away, and reread Uncle Henry's short note. He seemed just as confused by Dr. Parker's warnings about Dr. Harding as I was.

Although I've never met Harding, I'm sure he's quite sound. Multiple publications in all the best journals. Solid credentials. Of course, he apparently studied with Cope, who, as you now know, was Marsh's great rival in the rush to find dinosaur bones. And Parker has always been proud of his work with Marsh.

Uncle Henry wrote like he talked.

"It could be that Parker and Harding are fanning the flames of this old rivalry, although I doubt it," his note concluded. "I know Parker fairly well, and his only real shortcoming is an antiquated view of modern woman."

I smiled. Uncle Henry was still upset that Tom rather than Tabitha Fortune was working for Dr. Parker. But I was more worried about something else. If Dr. Harding had been associated with Dr. Cope, then he might be familiar with Mama's Badlands maps. I had the originals, but that didn't mean there weren't copies.

In the distance, I heard the wail of the 11:45. It was on time today. I slipped out the door, then broke into a run. The 11:45 had already pulled in and people were getting off. An old man with his little grand- daughter. A middle-aged man in a striped coat carry- ing a big black case—probably a traveling salesman. And a mother with twin babies and a toddler at her side. For a moment I wondered if Dr. Parker had made a mistake. Maybe Dr. Harding's assistant was coming later—on another train—or maybe he'd arrived early. There were so many people in town for Papa's sermon, I could have missed him.

Then a tall, bearded middle-aged man jumped off the train. He carried a satchel like Uncle Henry's and wore a well-cut suit of light wool. I heard him ask where he could find Mrs. Porter's café.

He waited on the platform for a set of battered leather suitcases, picked them up effortlessly, then walked down toward Sister Porter's. He hadn't seen me—I was standing behind the railing at the ticket counter—but there was something about him I liked. Maybe it was the way he moved. Maybe it was the satchel like Uncle Henry's. But, unlike Dr. Parker, this man looked like a dinosaur hunter should look. Fit. Rugged. Able.

*"Do not be misled by charm."*

Was that what Dr. Parker meant about Dr. Harding and the people who worked for him?

The man walked through town slowly. He stopped in front of the post office, then looked over at Luke's. He seemed to be sizing things up. He stopped again in front of Knudson's. Papa's church service had broken up, and people were lining up out in the street to shake Papa's hand. The man glanced up at the sign over Knudson's, said something to Buck Lowry, then crossed to Sister Porter's.

I hurried over and eased up to Buck. "Who was that?" I asked.

"Some stranger. Danged if he didn't want to know if the store was open for business on Sunday."

So, he needed to stock up on supplies. He had to be Dr. Harding's assistant. He'd probably hire a team from Luke's, then wire Dr. Harding right away. I started across toward Sister Porter's when Buck grabbed my arm.

"Then he asked about some *dinosaur* hunt. You know anything about that?"

I shook my head.

"Well, it's a shame your pa's goin' away Wednesday. I bet he'd put those dinosaur hunters in their place if'n he stayed."

# Chapter 19

His name was Charlie Curtis, and by noon the next day everyone in town knew he worked for A.V. Harding, world-famous dinosaur hunter. But they also knew that Dr. Harding wasn't the only dinosaur hunter coming to Rim. Dr. Phineas Parker, the *other* world-famous scientist, planned his own expedition.

I didn't want Curtis to buy up everything in town, so I had Abby confirm our orders for supplies, wagons, horses, and three teams of mules with Mr. Knudson and Luke. Abby had placed the orders back in April, saying that she had teamed up with old friends to do some prospecting in the Badlands. It wasn't a great story, but it was the best one I could think of at the time.

"They ain't buyin' my story no more, I kin tell ya that." Abby propped her feet up on her desk and shook her head. "But ain't nobody's cenneckted ya with this whole bizness jist yet."

"What about our supplies?"

"Good thing we laid some money down back in April, or we might not have them mules."

I telegraphed Dr. Parker that Curtis was in town, then went over to Luke's myself. I wanted to book Crow for the afternoon in case Curtis decided to do a little Badlands scouting for Dr. Harding.

Luke, standing with his back to me, was just outside the shadows of the big horse barn. At first I couldn't see who he was talking to. Then the man facing Luke stepped out through the wide double doorway. It was Curtis.

"Sure thing, Professor." I heard Luke's voice. "I can bring in two or three more mule teams and a couple a wagons by Friday, Saturday at the latest." He turned. "Why, Tabbie, have you met the good professor here?"

I shook my head, trying to appear calm, glad I was wearing one of my best waists and my good beige gabardine skirt. I couldn't have looked less like Tom Fortune.

"Tabbie here's one of our best and brightest," Luke boasted, putting his arm across my shoulder. "Tabitha Fortune, a schoolmarm now, the best in the whole state of South Dakota. Scored higher on her teachers examination than anyone else in the whole danged history of givin' out examinations."

Curtis smiled and shook my hand. It was a firm handshake. Sensible and strong. "Pleased to meet you, Miss Fortune."

"Saaay now." Luke took off his hat and scratched his

head. "You two have somethin' in common. Tabbie here knows a thing or two about them dinosaurs you're looking for, Professor." Luke's eyes twinkled. "Her pa don't think too highly of what she knows, but you might."

"Indeed?" Curtis looked at me squarely, and I wondered if he would react like Dr. Parker: "*Vertebrate paleontology is no place for a lady.*"

"Have you heard anything about Dr. Parker's plans, Miss Fortune?" Curtis asked. "Dr. Harding and I would prefer to join forces with Parker. We believe we could work more efficiently and effectively if we shared resources."

It sounded perfectly reasonable, but I remembered Dr. Parker's warnings about Dr. Harding's "unprofessional conduct" at the dig in Montana—and his orders to maintain secrecy.

"No, Professor Curtis, I'm afraid I can't help you."

I glanced over at Luke, who looked disappointed— and a little suspicious. He'd never known me to walk away from a chance to learn something new.

"But," I added, "I'd be very interested in your findings."

He lifted his hat in a polite good-bye. "Then perhaps you'll join us for a day's digging, Miss Fortune."

I gasped, unable to stop myself. An invitation to dig dinosaurs—as myself! Obviously, it didn't matter to Professor Curtis that I was a girl!

"*Do not be misled by charm.*"

I could almost hear Dr. Parker's warning ringing in

my ears. No, I had a job to do. I was working for Dr. Parker and I had to follow orders.

Professor Curtis walked away, then turned suddenly.

"We've heard through some of our contacts at Yale that Dr. Parker may have hired a local boy to do some scouting for him. Do you have any idea who that might be?"

I cleared my throat, hoping the color I felt rushing to my face wouldn't give me away. Still I couldn't find my voice. I just shook my head.

Professor Curtis looked disappointed.

"Say, Professor, you might wanna check over at the P. O.," Luke said slowly. "Don't know why I didn't think of it before." He chewed on a piece of straw. "Ask for Abby Hart. She *says* she's goin' prospectin' in the Badlands come Friday. But nobody's gone prospectin' in the Badlands fer years. She might be workin' for this here Dr. Parker."

"Thanks, Luke," he said. "I believe I *will* see your Abby Hart."

Professor Curtis tipped his hat to me, then crossed to the post office.

"Now, what can I do fer ya, Tabbie?" Luke asked.

I'd almost forgotten why I'd come. "Ah, I want to book Crow for the afternoon," I said, still watching Professor Curtis.

"The good professor there took one look at Crow and asked to book him for himself today." Luke spit out his piece of straw. "But I gave him Old Gray.

Crow's your horse for the whole summer, jist like I promised."

I tied up Crow and met Stephen on the front porch. He'd been waiting for me, I could tell.

"Heard about the dinosaur hunters, Tabbie?" he sneered. "Thought Papa might like to know about it before we go. He might want to take you with us if he finds out. Or maybe we wouldn't even go."

"Don't you dare tell Papa about this!"

"You can't stop me." Stephen swaggered toward Papa's study door.

Then I remembered something.

"Stephen," I said calmly. "You remember that day you went skinny-dipping last fall? Instead of going with me to Sally's? Papa might be very interested in your behavior on that occasion."

His face clouded. "That's not nearly as big as this," he said.

"Oh, I'm sure he'd be interested." I paused, watching Stephen's face closely. "I believe you owe me one." Stephen could be a jerk, but he had a strange sense of honor, his own code of ethics. It was the one thing about him that made me think he might turn out all right.

"Okay," he said finally. "But I won't do anything to *keep* Papa from finding out about it. I just won't say anything."

"Good." That was all I could ask. I'd just have to

hope that Papa kept himself occupied in his study, preparing sermons for his meetings with the elders in Kentucky.

I slipped into my room and changed into one of Artie's shirts, a pair of trousers, and the heavy, over-sized skirt Abby had given me. It was wide enough to camouflage my trousers, but it bunched up in layers at my waist when I cinched my belt tight. I strapped on my Smith & Wesson under the skirt and reached for my big cotton vest. It helped hide both my six-shooter and the wads of fabric at my waist. Then I crossed into the kitchen to fill my canteen. Papa's voice came through the study door like the rumble of distant thunder.

"Do you mean to tell me that in the midst of all these preparations for the most important journey of our lives, you have to see that old Indian woman tomor-row? She can wait until we get back."

"I have to see her, Charles," I heard Mama say. "She's ill."

I quietly closed the front door behind me, torn be-tween staying to help Mama and following Professor Curtis, who was obviously riding into the Badlands this afternoon. Glancing up the street toward Sister Porter's I saw Old Gray saddled out front. Tracking Professor Curtis was clearly more urgent.

I rode out of town, just beyond the first sandstone cliffs, and guided Crow behind a narrow outcropping. I slid out of the saddle, pulled off Abby's skirt, and stuffed it into a crevice. Then I loaded my revolver and waited for Professor Curtis. He'd have to come this way. It was the quickest, least treacherous passage into the Badlands from town.

Soon I heard Old Gray snort, and Professor Curtis reined him in about twenty feet away from my vantage point. He pulled out a map, studied it a few moments, and scanned the horizon. Then he folded it away and spurred Old Gray forward. The professor followed the trail southwest, toward the campsite I'd chosen for Dr. Parker. When Professor Curtis had rounded the first turn, I tucked my braid under my hat, swung into the saddle, and slowly urged Crow forward.

But Professor Curtis kept to the main track and didn't wind up the canyon trail toward our campsite. I felt I'd cleared the first hurdle. At least he wasn't using a copy of Mama's old maps.

The professor was fairly easy to follow. I held Crow back about a quarter of a mile behind Old Gray, and the twisting Badlands trail kept us out of the professor's sight. But it was also fairly easy to lose my concentration. The Badlands are radiant in June. Prickly pear, wallflower, and Spanish bayonet were in bloom. A ferruginous hawk circled overhead and its high scream echoed off the sheer sandstone walls. I wondered how dinosaurs had sounded. Did they roar? Or did they scream?

Suddenly everything seemed quiet. Too quiet. I slipped off Crow and led him through a series of hairpin turns. I stopped behind a low pile of rocks. The professor had dismounted, too. He ran his hands along a red formation, then reached for the pick he had strapped to the back of his saddle. He carefully chinked away at the stone. In just a few minutes, he'd cut away part of the rock. He held it up, turning it over slowly, then dropped it into the canvas bag he had slung around his shoulder. He pulled out his map again, then swung up on Old Gray. I watched him ride beyond a high, jagged wall before I followed on Crow.

Professor Curtis stopped two more times to examine formations and took another specimen at the last site. Then he turned off on the trail that headed up toward Sally's. I had to lag behind even farther because the country had opened up. But I saw him pass the turn to Sally's and move up even higher to a wide, grassy plateau. I guided Crow behind what Mama and I called Open Window, the last rocky formation my side of the plateau.

The professor dismounted slowly and walked over the wide, grassy tableland. I knew the ground there was smooth and even. A few ponderosa pines provided some shade. It was a perfect campsite. Almost. Because you'd have to haul in water all the way from town. The campsite I'd chosen for Dr. Parker was more efficient.

Professor Curtis started pacing off distances, maybe measuring the space between tents or where he wanted to set up an outdoor lab for bone preservation. After about fifteen or twenty minutes, he mounted Old Gray and headed back down the trail.

He was coming right toward me and Open Window, which from his new vantage point was no place for me to hide.

I guided Crow into rockier terrain, hoping the professor couldn't hear me and wouldn't notice Crow's prints. Just off the trail, I found a narrow ridge, perhaps ten feet high, and slipped behind it. I hoped Crow wouldn't whinny to Old Gray.

In minutes Professor Curtis was past Open Window and coming right toward me. I held my breath. He passed so close I could see the wrinkles under his eyes.

Then he was gone, cantering back to the spot where he'd taken his last specimen. He was there almost an hour, deliberately chipping away rock. It even looked like he made extensive notes before he left.

I waited until I couldn't hear the sound of Old Gray's hoofbeats, then spurred Crow onto the trail and stopped at the formation the professor had studied so carefully. I slipped from the saddle and knelt by the red sandstone wall.

And there it was. Eight inches of exposed bone. My hand trembled as I ran my fingers along the slightly arched remains of an animal long dead. Dead hundreds of thousands of years. A dinosaur perhaps. *Triceratops* or *Iguanodon* or *Dimetredon*.

I pulled out the small sketchbook I now took with me everywhere and copied the outline of the bone for Dr. Parker. I felt certain Professor Curtis and Dr. Harding would dig here, but how would it compare to the site I had found for Dr. Parker?

Rocky shadows cut across the trail as I spurred Crow

back toward town. I knew Professor Curtis was way
ahead of me now, moving quickly. By the time I
reached the last wall of rock, the professor and Old
Gray were moving specks in a sea of grass, the town a
little clump of gray just ahead of them.

As I slid off, Crow tried to shake the saddle from his
back. I stroked his broad neck, thankful for such a
sure-footed, quiet animal. I pulled off my hat and my
braid swung free. Then I unloaded my revolver and
reached for my skirt, rolled up in the shallow crevice.

I pulled it out and a small piece of rock clattered to
my feet.

Sandstone. Red sandstone. Six inches long, three
inches wide.

I picked it up and turned it over slowly in my hands,
its fossil outline clear and sharp and clean. A calling
card from the professor.

# *Chapter* 20

Papa was still in the study the next morning when Luke arrived with Crow and Ransom, the only horse Luke owned that he never rented out—except to Mama.

"Good morning, Luke," Mama said, carrying her picnic hamper on her elbow. "Thank you for bringing the horses around."

I strapped two bolts of cotton and a case of Sally's eyedrops to the back of Crow's saddle.

"Surprised you're headed out to ole Sally's." Luke draped Ransom's reins over the hitching post out front. "You and the Reverend leavin' tomarrah and all."

"We'll be back early this afternoon, Luke," said Mama. He helped her into the saddle, something else he did only for Mama.

He tipped his hat. "You be careful out there, Miz Fortune." Then he laughed. "Don't let any of them *dinosaurs* catch ya." He winked at me and ambled up the street.

"What did he mean by that?" Papa's voice boomed

out. He stood on the front porch, hands behind his back, his face haggard from too much sermon-writing.

I tried to think fast. "You know Luke, Papa. Always teasing me about dinosaurs—ever since your sermon last year." Papa and I had never talked about that sermon, but now it didn't bother me anymore.

Papa raised an eyebrow, but he didn't ask any more questions. Apparently he still didn't know about Professor Curtis and Dr. Parker. So Stephen had kept his promise.

"We should be home early this afternoon, Charles. I've left you and Stephen cold chicken for lunch." Mama's voice sounded cool, detached. "You should be able to manage just fine without me."

Then she glanced over at me. "Let's go, Tabitha." She spurred Ransom and cantered out toward the Badlands.

Papa leaned against the porch railing and for a moment he seemed frail and tired. He brushed his hand across his eyes, then straightened. "Go with your mother, Daughter," his voice suddenly stern but soft. "You're two of a kind."

It was a beautiful morning. The sky was bright, bright blue with layers of thin, flat clouds hanging high over the Badlands. Prairie dogs scolded us as we headed down a smooth stretch of trail. A red-winged blackbird flickered past. I wondered suddenly if dinosaurs had such distinctive markings, bright bands of color like the exotic birds or lizards in the pictures I'd seen in Uncle Henry's books. Fossilized bones showed us so much—and so little.

I reached for the professor's fossil in my shallow vest pocket. I had studied it carefully the night before, and I felt sure it was all that remained of a Cretaceous willow. It was very much like the willows that clustered around White River. But I wondered what it really meant, almost afraid to admit my worst fear: That the professor knew I was "the boy" working for Dr. Parker.

Mama and I were halfway to Sally's, perhaps a quarter of a mile from the formation where the professor had spent so much time the day before. I felt certain he would be there this morning.

Mama slowed Ransom to a walk. "What *did* Luke mean this morning, Tabitha?" Mama's hat shaded her eyes. "Why did he mention dinosaurs?"

I reined Crow in. Perhaps it was time to tell Mama the whole truth.

"Two teams of paleontologists are going to dig for dinosaur bones here this summer." Now Mama's entire face was shaded by her hat. "A Professor Curtis is already in town working for someone named Dr. Harding. Dr. Parker, who spoke at the Corn Palace last year, will be here on Friday. The whole town's talking about it."

Mama pulled up on the reins and Ransom came to a complete stop. "Are you involved in this?"

The wind whistled through the canyon.

"Yes," I said slowly. "I'm working for Dr. Parker."

Mama nodded. She turned and faced me squarely. Her eyes looked sad but sympathetic. "That explains a lot."

She spurred Ransom into an easy canter and I followed, clearing the last bend in the trail before reaching the professor's excavation. I saw Old Gray before I saw the professor.

"Hello there, ladies!" he called out. "What brings you out into this wilderness on such a fine June morning?" He tossed his pick aside and brushed his hands on his trousers.

"You must be one of the paleontologists Tabitha just told me about," Mama said evenly.

Professor Curtis grinned at me. "Ah, Miss Fortune. I didn't recognize you at first."

I nodded slowly, feeling the blood rush to my face. Had he emphasized the word *recognize*—or was it my imagination? The fossil in my vest pocket suddenly felt heavy.

"Mama, this is Professor Curtis, who works for *Dr. Harding*."

Mama glanced at me. "I see," she said. "And what have you found today, Professor Curtis? It looks as though you've already spent a great deal of time here."

Mama was right. Yesterday eight inches had been cut away. Now another eight inches of bone had been exposed. I edged Crow closer to the rock wall. The bone looked like a rib curving into the rock.

"It looks like we may have at least part of a *Triceratops*, a horned plant-eater." The professor followed the outline of the bone with his fingertips. "Obviously, I'll make more progress once Dr. Harding and the rest of our crew arrives Sunday."

I was surprised at the professor's candor. Maybe he didn't suspect me. Or maybe he didn't care.

"I wish you the best of luck then, Professor Curtis." Mama eased Ransom ahead and motioned for me to follow.

"Good-bye, Miss Fortune." Professor Curtis raised his hat. "Until our paths cross again."

He *did* suspect me! I felt it as surely as heat in August. But would he keep my secret?

Mama and I passed Open Window, then headed up toward Sally's. The sky was perfectly clear now, except for a low, thin row of clouds hanging way, way out west toward the Black Hills.

"Does the professor know you're working for Dr. Parker?" Mama asked.

"I'm not sure. I've tried to keep it a secret. No one knows—except for Abby. She's working for Dr. Parker, too."

Mama urged Ransom up the last broad incline before we reached Sally's. "A wise choice." Mama smiled. "Nobody keeps a secret better than Abby Hart—unless it's Sally Dancing Moon."

I could just make out Sally's cabin and tipi in the distance. Her grandson's pony was tied up out front.

Maybe there was more to this illness than we thought. After all, Ned was a medical student at Vermillion. He met us by the tipi.

"Is it serious this time, Ned?" Mama asked, gracefully swinging out of the saddle.

He cocked an eyebrow. "She claims she's dying."

Mama and I both sighed with relief. Sally had said she was going to die at least half a dozen times since I'd known her.

"It is time to die," she'd say. "My husband's spirit calls to me." She'd lie in her bed maybe a week or two, demanding attention from her family—or Mama—until she got tired of dying. Then she'd send everyone packing—without any apologies.

"If you've brought fried chicken," Ned continued, "Grandmother may make an amazing recovery in the next hour."

"Just what the doctor ordered." Mama unstrapped the picnic basket and handed it to Ned. I followed with Sally's supplies.

Inside, the cabin was dark, cool, and cramped. The bed was pushed against the far wall.

"What took you so long?" Sally demanded. "I expected you yesterday."

She was propped up in bed, her favorite star quilt tucked up to her chin. She *did* look weak, but I knew Sally could be a very convincing actress when it suited her.

Mama sat in a chair beside the bed and pulled Sally's hand out from under her quilt.

"What's the matter with you now, Sally?" Mama sighed.

"I hear my husband's spirit calling to me," she crooned, rocking back and forth. "It is my time to die." She opened one eye and looked first at Mama, then at me.

I exchanged glances with Ned and tried not to smile. No, there was nothing wrong with Sally; she was plainly up to her old tricks again.

Then suddenly she turned and squinted at me.

"One Who Goes Among Ghosts," she whispered, pointing a bony finger in my direction, "they have heard you calling. Yes, they have heard you calling. But they will not come until your heart is clear."

# Chapter 21

"It's positively providential," Sister Porter babbled over the train whistle. Her face beamed as she shook Mama's hand, then Papa's. "The way these dinosaur hunters have come to town just when you folks are leavin'. And all of us here so worried about business now that people won't be comin' to hear you preach, Reverend." The train pulled in and sent out a blast of steam. "But we shouldn't a worried. These dinosaur hunters are pickin' up the slack."

Papa's face clouded. "Dinosaur hunters?" He looked at Mama, then at me.

I held my breath, wishing Sister Porter would shut up. Stephen smirked at me over Mama's shoulder.

"You know," Sister Porter gushed on, "those scientists from back East. The whole town's just crawling with 'em."

"All aboard!" the conductor's voice rang down the platform.

"Come on, Charles. We can't miss our train." Mama

gathered me in her arms. "Good luck," she whispered, as she kissed me good-bye.

But Papa stood perfectly still on the platform.

"Dorothy, did you know about this?"

"What, Charles?" She shoved Stephen in my direction for a farewell hug.

"Dinosaur hunters." Papa's voice rose. "Evolutionists. Here in Rim."

Mama reached for her carpetbag, then took Papa's arm and nudged him toward the train. "They'll make a fine topic for your next sermon just as soon as we get back. I'm sure Tabitha would be happy to take any notes you might need for it."

She and Papa took two or three steps, then Papa turned. His eyes narrowed as he looked at me. "I'm sure she would," he said.

Then they were on the train, Stephen waving out the window, Mama and Papa silhouetted against the glass.

The train lurched forward. Slowly. Slowly.

They were going and I was free!

Suddenly Papa spun out of his seat and ran back down the aisle, toward the door. But the train gained momentum and slowly, slowly pulled clear of the platform, clear of the depot. Papa leaned out the door, one arm raised, and yelled something at me.

Then the train rounded a curve and Papa was gone.

\*    \*    \*

Abby and I spent the afternoon and the next morning setting up camp at the spot Tom Fortune used for target practice. Then we rode to the excavation site to test the ramp Jesse had built over the lowest point in Ghost Horse Canyon, that pink sandstone dollop I'd found last November.

The ramp squeaked and groaned, but it held, even with a full wagon-load of supplies and a team of four mules. It took us nearly two hours to get back to camp, but nothing in our wagon was damaged. I felt sure Dr. Parker would approve.

We sat in front of Abby's cook tent at sunset, drinking coffee she'd brewed from the stock pond.

"Yer a right smart girl, Tabbie. Thinkin' a that ramp 'n all. Right smart." She emptied her tin cup and leaned forward on one knee. "Pity ya have to be a boy to do it, though."

Abby reached into her vest pocket and pulled out a pair of mustache scissors. She wiped her hands on her skirt. "Ready to take off that braid?"

I fingered my long black braid tenderly.

"Let's not cut it yet," I said. "Tom still needs to have his sister around for a few more days." I had decided to meet Dr. Parker in town the next day as Tabitha; I wasn't comfortable assuming my disguise in town.

Abby frowned. "Yer runnin' an awful risk. That braid jist has to flop outta yer hat one time and yer done fer, Tom Fortune."

"I have to be Tabitha for the folks in town. It just

takes one person to talk, Abby, and then I'm really done for." I could almost hear Sister Porter say, "Tom Fortune? Never heard of him."

Abby stared at me a minute or two, then lit a cigar. She settled into her camp stool.

"I see the point of it," she said at last. "Should a thought of it myself."

I grinned at Abby. "Thanks." I valued her opinion more than anybody's.

Abby stretched out her legs. Her spurs jingled. "So, it begins tomarrah," she whispered, blowing a smoke ring toward the twilight's first pale, distant star.

I nodded and looked out at the Badlands, glittering purple, gold, and blue against a crimson sky. There were butterflies in my stomach; I couldn't wait for the next day to get here. But there was a darker thought, too. A feeling that something wasn't right. I pulled out my notepad and reviewed my final notes for the day. Nothing was missing. I was as ready as I'd ever be.

*Too ready*, I thought suddenly.

I got to my feet and walked out to the edge of camp. A red half-sun glimmered in the stock pond. A lone Canada goose glided across its surface. What if that was a buffalo bone in Ghost Horse Canyon? Or a prehistoric camel or horse?

"Dinosaurs rather than extinct mammals are our objective," Dr. Parker had written.

So then what would I do if we found only mammals in the canyon? If the first site didn't work out, where would I lead Dr. Parker and his crew?

I hadn't seen Professor Curtis two for days. It was as if the Badlands had swallowed him up. Luke didn't even know where he'd gone. All he could say was that Dr. Harding himself would be in town the following week.

I took out the professor's fossil and turned it over in my hands. I'd bet Professor Curtis had backup plans for Dr. Harding. But then the professor already *knew* he'd found a dinosaur bone. When would I have that kind of knowledge?

I thought I heard Sally Dancing Moon laughing. *"They will come when your heart is clear."*

But it was just the wind.

# Chapter 22

Dr. Parker emerged from the train looking hot and flustered in a white linen suit that was two sizes too small across the middle. He took off his large Panama hat and wiped his forehead with a white handkerchief.

Abby nudged my back and pointed to Dr. Parker. "Who's that?"

"That's him."

Abby spit a big wad of tobacco toward the platform and wrinkled up her face. "Not exactly a fine figur' of a man, now, is he?"

I couldn't help sharing her disappointment. His skin was pastier, smoother than I'd remembered. I hated to admit it, but I wished Dr. Parker looked more robust, like Professor Curtis.

Dr. Parker turned back toward the train and barked a command to a man standing behind him. Probably Bill Seymour, an expert in fossil preparation techniques. The rest of Dr. Parker's crew—the three graduate students—weren't due until Sunday, the same day I believed Dr. Harding would arrive.

"I don't think he's seen ya, Tabbie." Abby nodded toward the platform. "Anyway, he don't look too happy right now."

Dr. Parker squinted into the distance and stuck out his lower lip. Maybe he was looking for Tom.

I walked up to the platform and held out a gloved hand, hoping to look dainty and demure, everything Tom Fortune was not.

"Remember me, Dr. Parker?" I asked sweetly. "I'm Tabitha Fortune. Tom's sister."

"Miss Fortune! What a surprise." He swept off his broad hat and took my hand.

"Welcome to Rim." I smiled and tilted my head, just like Artie's friend Janette Becker.

Dr. Parker stood on tiptoe and looked over my shoulder. "Where's that brother of yours? Isn't he here?"

"He's back at base camp."

"Highly irregular," Dr. Parker growled.

"He stayed," I improvised quickly, "to make sure Professor Curtis didn't get too close to your operation."

Dr. Parker smiled slowly, then turned to Bill Seymour, a lean, wiry-looking man with watery eyes. "I told you this young Fortune was a good find. Very discreet."

We moved down the platform and Mr. Seymour gave the porter instructions about their trunks. Abby was waiting with her buckboard right below us. She climbed out of the wagon, revealing the buckskin pants under her khaki skirt. Dr. Parker wrinkled his nose.

"Howdy, sir." Abby wiped her hand on her skirt, then held it out for Dr. Parker. "A pleasure to meet ya after all these months."

He took her hand gingerly, and I remembered Uncle Henry's warning: "Parker believes women should stay at home." Abby certainly didn't fit the Parker ideal of womanhood.

"Limp handshake," she whispered. "A bit of a dandy, I'd say. Let's hope he improves once he gits close to them dinosaur bones ya found fer him."

I watched Dr. Parker fussing with his trunks, waving a complicated set of loading directions to the porter and Mr. Seymour.

"Remember, Abby," I said. "He's a brilliant and respected scientist. Give him a chance."

Abby spit a wad of tobacco and winked. "I've seen worse."

The trunks were finally loaded to Dr. Parker's satisfaction. Bill Seymour jumped into the wagon next to Abby, then helped Dr. Parker up.

"Mr. Seymour could drive us out to camp if you prefer," Dr. Parker puffed, as Abby took the reins.

"Nonsense, Doc," Abby replied, spitting another wad of tobacco.

Dr. Parker cringed and watched Abby's wad arch over the side of the wagon. His face turned pale green. Abby could brew camp coffee and fry eggs off a Badlands bluff if she had to, but I could see it was going to be a long time before Dr. Parker appreciated her finer points.

I held up my hand and smiled like Janette one more time. "Your horses and three teams of mules are back at camp with Tom. But this is where I leave you, sir. And I leave you in good hands. Abby's the best driver west of the Missouri."

Dr. Parker smiled weakly. "We shall see, Miss Fortune."

I turned to Abby, "Give Tom my love;" then whispered, "Be sure to drive really slow."

"Well, good luck, Dr. Parker," I said, slowly backing away from the wagon. For some strange reason, I found myself hoping he would invite me—Tabitha—to dig dinosaurs with him and Mr. Seymour, like Professor Curtis had done. But the moment passed. Dr. Parker tipped his hat and nodded good-bye.

I stood waving until the wagon passed our house at the edge of town, then ran home, tore off my clothes, and jumped into my Tom Fortune outfit. Crow was saddled out back. I spurred him into a full gallop.

I reined him in by a sandstone outcropping when I spotted them. Abby was following our plan. She'd driven out by the first stock pond just beyond town and was standing in the wagon, pointing west, toward the Black Hills. "Orientin' them to their new surroundin's," as she had promised.

Crow and I easily slipped past them and raced toward base camp.

*   *   *

Jesse met me outside Abby's cook tent, and I thanked him for guarding the place while I was in town meeting Dr. Parker. He grunted, then reached into his pocket and pulled out a letter.

"I shoulda give it to ya last night," he said, and shuffled over to his horse.

I glanced down at the envelope. BECKER DRUG EMPORIUM. His timing couldn't have been better! I needed a little encouragement before Tom Fortune made his first real appearance.

I followed Jesse to his horse. "Any visitors?" I asked, wondering if Professor Curtis had come by to check on our operation—or to see Dr. Parker.

"Nope."

I glanced around the camp. The horses and mules were tethered. The tents were pitched in a neat row: two for Dr. Parker and Bill Seymour, two for his graduate assistants, Abby's cook tent, and mine on the other side. The supplies were neatly arranged under a canvas tarp.

"Thanks again, Jesse. I couldn't have done all this without you."

He smiled. "Good luck, Tom. See ya around."

Jesse spurred his horse into a slow canter and was gone.

I walked to the stock pond and leaned against a lone, scraggly cottonwood. Still no sign of Abby and the wagon. I tore into Artie's letter.

Dear Tabbie,

Or is it already Tom?

You've probably found your first dinosaur by now and impressed old Parker as a great scout, sharpshooter, and scientist. Won't he be surprised when he finds out who you really are—if he finds out. Dad says he may come out later this month to see how things are going. But I said you won't need any help. With you around, Dr. Parker is sure to make a major discovery.

I have big news myself and that's why I'm writing. I want you to be the first to know.

I'm going to marry Janette Becker. Not right away—not until I'm twenty-one. By that time, I should be a partner in her father's store, and my future will be secure.

I want you and Janette to be friends. Please give her a chance—for me. Can you come for the Corn Palace Festival? We're planning a big engagement party and I'd like you to be there.

Good luck, Tom. Write me about your adventures.

Artie

*Engaged!* But his life had barely started! He'd just turned eighteen last month.

I crumpled the letter in my fist and stared out across the stock pond, wanting to cry, knowing I couldn't.

*"When I became a man, I put away childish things."*

Artie had quoted that to me last year in Mitchell.

Suddenly I thought of Mama, trading her book for a life with Papa. She had quoted that passage, too.

"Hey, Tom! We're here!"

I stuffed the letter in my pocket and strode over to the tents, conscious of the way I walked.

Like Artie did.

# *Chapter 23*

"Fortune! At last we meet." Dr. Parker studied me closely. "Amazing resemblance to your sister. But isn't it a curious fact of science, that those features that appear pleasing in a woman are so much stronger, more developed in a man. Don't you agree, Seymour?"

I shook hands with Bill Seymour, trying not to laugh as Abby shook her head and spit.

Seymour eyed me suspiciously. "So, Fortune," he grunted. His eyes lingered on mine, then his gaze moved up to my hat. "You look a lot like your sister, boy. That's all I can say."

I gave him my best Artie Winslow handshake, then turned and caught up with Dr. Parker, who was moving down the row of tents.

"Your tent, sir." I pointed to the largest of four tents just south of Abby's. "Mr. Seymour's is next to yours. These two are for your assistants, and mine is the small one just north of the cook tent. I wanted to be close to the supplies and livestock."

"Fine work, Fortune." Dr. Parker surveyed the camp, his eyes resting on the stock pond.

"Dern good thing we don't have to haul water," Seymour grumbled from behind.

Dr. Parker nodded. "Fine work," he repeated. "Very fine." He turned, clasping his hands behind his back, and paced toward Abby's tent. "Any sign of our rivals?" he asked.

"Professor Curtis has set up camp about eight miles southwest of us," I said, pointing over the stock pond. "They'll have to haul their water in."

"Good." Dr. Parker smiled, rubbing his hands together. "Hear that, Bill? Harding will have to haul water in. A.V. won't like that." He snickered, then whispered confidentially, "Two years ago, Harding hauled a bathtub cross-country. Took bubble baths at the end of every day's digging." Dr. Parker shuddered. "What has science come to?"

It was a rather shocking luxury, but was that the only reason Dr. Parker didn't want to work with Dr. Harding? Was that the "unprofessional conduct" he'd hinted at in his letters? Surely there had to be something more. I pulled out the drawing I'd made of the fossils Professor Curtis was carving out of the sandstone wall near Sally's.

"Their base camp may not be as efficient as ours, sir, but I think their main excavation area is very promising."

"How did you get this?" Seymour looked me over

from my boots up, his gaze lingering once again on my hat. I felt like he was sizing me up, still not sure what to make of me. Maybe he did suspect me.

I shifted my weight the way Artie sometimes does before answering a question, and looked straight at Bill Seymour. "I followed Professor Curtis on one of his scouting missions."

"Did Curtis see you?" Dr. Parker asked, squinting at my drawing.

I fingered the professor's fossil in my pocket. "I'm not sure," I admitted. "But he gave my sister this." I handed it to Dr. Parker.

"Your sister?" He shook his head, glancing at Seymour. "Curtis is such a charmer." Then he turned back toward me. "I hope your sister had the good sense not to be impressed." He tossed the fossil on the ground, then bent to look closer at my drawing.

"What do you make of it, Phin?" Bill Seymour looked over my shoulder. His eyes narrowed as he studied the sketch. "Nice work, kid," he said slowly.

I tipped my hat back slightly. "Professor Curtis has tentatively identified it as a *Triceratops*," I said, "maybe even a new species."

"I can't confirm what he's found from this drawing. I'd need to see it." Dr. Parker handed my sketch back, but he looked worried.

"When did you say Harding was getting here?" Seymour asked.

"Day after tomorrow. Anyway, that's my best guess," I said.

Seymour pursed his lips and nodded. His eyes met Dr. Parker's.

"My thoughts exactly, Bill." Dr. Parker chuckled. "We can ride over, take a look at what Curtis has found, *and* get back here while Curtis is meeting the splendid Dr. Harding at the depot. Can you take us there, Thomas?"

I felt a little uncomfortable with Dr. Parker's idea. I'd already spied on Professor Curtis, even sketched what he'd found. But spying seemed a little unethical for someone as important as Dr. Parker to do. Besides, he'd be outraged if Professor Curtis or Dr. Harding spied on us.

"Why not ride out tomorrow?" I suggested. "Talk to Professor Curtis ourselves. He's already said he and Dr. Harding would like to share information with us."

Bill Seymour threw back his head and laughed. "This is war, kid. To the victor go the spoils. Or should I say, the fossils?"

He turned and ground the professor's fossil fragment into the dirt.

I looked up at Abby, who stood outside the cook tent. She'd probably heard the entire conversation. She spit a wad of tobacco in Bill Seymour's direction.

"Lone rider, comin' our way," she said. She pointed to a cloud of dust below us. "Be here faster 'n greased lightnin'."

I squinted into the sun. The horse was Old Gray; the rider had to be Professor Curtis.

Seymour reached for his shotgun and walked beyond the row of tents. He held the gun across his body, balanced lightly in both hands. He looked more like a sheriff than a fossil preparator.

"Well, Curtis. Long time no see," Seymour said, as the professor rode into camp.

Professor Curtis swung out of the saddle. "Good to see you, Bill," he said easily. "Where's your boss?"

Dr. Parker stepped out from behind his tent. He held out his hand stiffly. "Charlie," he said.

They shook hands, but I could tell it was a courtesy Dr. Parker didn't enjoy.

"I was collecting over in the next valley." Professor Curtis grinned. "I thought I'd be neighborly and invite you over to see what I've found. *Triceratops*. Possibly an entire skeleton."

I gasped. It was such a decent thing to do. I glanced over at Abby, who nodded in approval. Bubble bath or no, Professor Curtis, as a representative for Dr. Harding, was acting more like a professional than Dr. Parker and Bill Seymour.

"A commendable idea, Charlie," said Dr. Parker smoothly, though his face had suddenly turned red. "When would you like us?"

"Bright and early in the morning. Say, seven-thirty?"

Dr. Parker nodded. "Seven-thirty it is."

"I think your scout probably knows the way." Professor Curtis grinned again and looked right at me. "I met his mother and sister a few days ago. I'm sure they told him all about it."

"Yes." Dr. Parker's chest swelled out a little. "Thomas here told us you may have uncovered a new species. So you see, your news isn't really news at all. Still, I'm eager to see this new species of yours for myself." His words had a sting to them that reminded me of Papa's sermons. Dr. Parker took Seymour's arm and turned back toward camp. "We'll see you in the morning, then," he said over his shoulder. "Seven-thirty."

Professor Curtis mounted Old Gray. He glanced at Abby, then back at me.

"Good day, Miss Fortune," he whispered. "A pleasure seeing you again."

# *Chapter* 24

"Hadrosaur tibia," Dr. Parker murmured, running his hands along the exposed bone in Ghost Horse Canyon.

I wanted to jump and shout and dance. It *was* a dinosaur, not a mammal! But I stood still, taking the news like a man, waiting for a handshake or a slap on the back.

But when Dr. Parker turned to look at me, his eyes were veiled, his voice thick with disappointment. "I'd hoped for a carnivore. They're much more rare."

Seymour nodded. "Doesn't look like anything new, but it's too soon to tell."

Dr. Parker had asked for dinosaur bones and I'd found them. Yet that didn't seem to be enough. Apparently, what he really wanted was a new species, a carnivore that he alone could claim. This morning at Professor Curtis's site, Dr. Parker and Seymour had pretended not to be impressed with the professor's *Triceratops*, but I knew they believed he had found a new species. And that worried them.

"You've done a commendable job, Thomas. Very commendable." Dr. Parker took off his coat and reached for a bag of tools. "The wagon ramp is a brilliant idea."

Somehow his praise seemed weak.

Seymour took a pick out of the wagon and set to work.

I offered to help. This was my first dinosaur. I wanted to unearth it, wrap its bones in gauze and plaster, load it gently on the wagon, take it safely across the ramp myself. It was my hadrosaur, even if Dr. Parker didn't believe it was significant.

"Do some more scouting, kid," Seymour said with his back to me. "If this site doesn't pan out, we'll need another one."

I backed away. *Boys don't cry*, I told myself.

"Yes," Dr. Parker called out. "By all means. And be sure to keep Charlie Curtis out of here."


I drew myself up tight against the shadowed east wall of the depot, hoping for a glimpse of Dr. A. V. Harding before Dr. Parker's graduate students got off the train. But the 3:24 from Pierre was late, very late. And I was beginning to feel vulnerable. I'd been in town for over an hour dressed as Tom Fortune. No one had noticed me yet, but I wasn't sure how much longer I could push my luck. I pulled my pocket watch from my vest. Six-thirty. If the train were much later, I'd have to take Dr. Parker's assistants to base camp after dark. That could be interesting.

More interesting than the last day and a half of unsuccessful scouting, anyway.

"Tom!" a voice called.

I flattened against the wall, hoping the shadows would hide me.

"Tom!" the voice came again.

Jesse Hart peered around the corner and thrust a yellow Western Union envelope in my direction.

I opened it slowly.

> DELAYED. ARRIVE TOMORROW. 324.
> YALE PALEO ASSTS.

"Thanks, Jesse."

I folded the telegram into my pocket and looked up the tracks. There was the 3:24, whistle blowing, great puffs of steam swirling around the engine. Would Dr. Harding be on it? I glanced up Main, looking for Professor Curtis. He wasn't anywhere in sight. But Mr. Knudson and Sister Porter came trotting up toward the depot. I stepped deeper into the shadows.

Only a few people got off the train: Sister Porter's sickly niece and her two little boys; a stout old man in a shiny black suit carrying a traveling salesman's bag; and a fashionably dressed woman, small and plump like Janette, in an elegant traveling costume of buttery linen. The conductor handed Mr. Knudson a special delivery box, then called out, "All aboard!"

The stout old man claimed his trunk and followed Sister Porter and her niece down the street. The fashionably dressed woman readjusted her gloves and paced across the platform like the caged lioness I'd seen once at a circus in Mitchell.

Maybe Dr. Harding had been delayed with Dr. Parker's graduate assistants. I flipped open my pocket watch. Seven o'clock. If I hurried, I'd just make it back to camp before dark.

As I turned to go, I saw Professor Curtis jump out of his wagon. He hurried up to the platform

"A.V.!" he called. "A.V.!"

The woman on the platform turned and smiled.

# *Chapter* 25

"Where's Peterson?" Professor Curtis asked, loading the first of Dr. Harding's trunks into the back of the wagon.

Dr. Harding dragged the second trunk to the edge of the platform. "Came down with the mumps in Sioux City. Not a pretty sight."

"We'll be shorthanded then." Professor Curtis grunted as he hoisted up the second trunk. "What about Colby?"

I edged closer.

Dr. Harding jumped off the platform. Her high-heeled boots dug little holes in the dirt where she walked.

"I wired him from Pierre. His father died suddenly. Colby won't join us until August." She climbed into the wagon. "But there's a swarm of graduate students coming in tomorrow to work for old Phin. Maybe we could lure a few away from the fold."

Professor Curtis turned my way. I ducked around the corner of the depot—too late.

"Miss Fortune!" he called. "Miss Fortune."

He jumped up on the platform and grabbed my arm. "Come here. Let me introduce you to Dr. Annabelle V. Harding." He pulled me toward the wagon. "This is the young woman I wrote you about. Tabitha Fortune."

I took off my hat, letting my braid swing free, and Dr. Harding held out a gloved hand. A thin bracelet of garnets hung loosely around her wrist.

"Please call me A. V. Any woman who works for Dr. Phineas Parker has my complete admiration." She smiled and her dimples reminded me of Janette Becker's. Dr. Harding was so feminine, so utterly fashionable. "The wonder is," Dr. Harding continued, "how you fooled him." Her eyes ran over my face and hair. "Still, Parker can be blind as a bat, especially when faced with the obvious."

There was something about Dr. Harding I liked. An air of self-confidence and honesty. She and Abby couldn't be more different, and yet they were alike somehow.

"It's a pleasure to meet you," I managed to say, still holding my hat in my hand. "I was here to meet Dr. Parker's graduate assistants, but they've been delayed."

"And you were probably spying on me." She winked at Professor Curtis.

I started to protest, but she interrupted. "I admire your guts, Miss Fortune. You've done what you've had to do."

She opened a buttery lace parasol that perfectly matched the rest of her costume. "But be advised, *Mr.* Fortune, you'll have a tougher time fooling Dr. Parker's assistants than you've had with the Great Phin. Boys will be boys. And they can recognize a young lady a mile away."

Professor Curtis jumped into the wagon and took the reins. "My invitation still holds, *Miss* Fortune," he said. "You're welcome to work with us anytime."

"And since we're shorthanded," Dr. Harding added, "I'll meet Parker's salary and add an extra two dollars a week. Think about it."

Professor Curtis clicked to the mules, and the wagon moved up the street past our house, then out into the glittering Badlands.

I walked toward Luke's. I needed time alone. Time to think. Maybe I could slip into the loft for a little while. I darted through the wide back doors and climbed up. It wasn't too hot, and the smell of hay and leather and horses was comforting. Like old times— those afternoons when I'd escape here to read Uncle Henry's books in secret. I lay back and closed my eyes.

Annabelle V. Harding. She was doing what I'd always wanted to do. But was she legitimate, respected? I recalled what Uncle Henry had written. "I'm sure Harding's quite sound. Multiple publications in all the best journals. Solid credentials." But Uncle Henry hadn't known Dr. Harding was a woman. Or had he?

Maybe it didn't matter. But with a name like A.V., she certainly didn't *sound* like a woman.

Now Dr. Parker's letters—and his behavior—were beginning to make sense. He considered Dr. Harding a monstrosity. I rolled over on my stomach and chewed on a piece of straw. Still, I'd signed on with Dr. Parker, and I felt I owed him my allegiance. I couldn't abandon my post just because A.V. Harding was a woman. That wouldn't be professional.

"Tabbie? Tabbie? Are you up there?" Luke looked up at me from the barn floor.

"Say, Luke, I need to talk to you."

I brushed the straw off my clothes and shimmied down the ladder.

"Tabbie," he said, sizing me up, taking in everything from my boots to my trousers to my hat. "You workin' with them scientists after all?"

I nodded.

"Thought so all along." Luke seemed happy, even proud. "Cain't keep a girl like you down no ways."

"Look, Abby won't need these horses till tomorrow." I pointed to the three saddle horses tied up out front. "Dr. Parker's assistants have been delayed a day."

We walked out into the street and Luke took my arm. He pointed across to the post office. "Ned Dancing Moon's in town. Lookin' for your ma."

## Chapter 26

Sally was buried two days later. I stood next to Ned, high on Sally's windswept butte, after everyone else had gone. A dry wind whipped through the ponderosa pines, scattering the bouquets of crazyweed and western wallflower left on Sally's grave. The sun was low in the sky, the shadows across the Badlands were long. But I didn't want to leave.

"Thank you for reading your mother's message," Ned said finally. "Her words meant a great deal to my family."

I nodded. Ned's father had wanted Mama to speak at the funeral. Since she couldn't be here, Mama had telegrammed to suggest that I read a story from her book, "The Girl Who Walks Two Paths." Sally's favorite. It was a sad story about a girl whose people always quarreled and forced her to make a choice between those who sided with her parents and those who sided with her brave young lover. She walked down both paths, becoming two girls. One dark. One light.

But her spirit craved unity, and when she died, her people were finally united in their grief.

I turned back toward Ned. He took my hand and I knew it was time to go. We started back down toward Sally's hut when two riders topped the crest of the butte. A man and a woman.

I squinted. Professor Curtis and . . . Dr. Harding?

"Do you know these people?" Ned's voice was low.

I nodded. "But I don't know why they're here."

Dr. Harding slowly dismounted and unstrapped a huge bouquet of wild penstemon from the back of her saddle. She was tiny up close, a small woman dressed in khaki, the mounds of puffed-up hair I'd seen in Rim now braided tight and thick down her back. She didn't look at all like the woman I'd met in town—except for her walk. Sure and straight and forceful. She walked right up to Ned.

"You must be Mrs. Dancing Moon's grandson," she said, her voice more tender than I remembered.

Ned nodded and took the flowers Dr. Harding offered.

"I'm Annabelle Harding. I met your grandmother several years ago. I was an assistant on a dinosaur dig here with Dr. Cope. Your grandmother was very kind to all of us."

I stopped short. Dr. Harding had been part of Dr. Cope's Badlands expedition! If she knew Sally, she must have known Mama, too.

Dr. Harding and Ned turned and walked back toward Sally's grave. "I hope you don't mind," she was saying, "that I've come to pay my respects."

At that moment, I looked up at Professor Curtis, still mounted on his horse. The professor lifted his hat and smiled.

Suddenly it hit me, and I couldn't smile back.

Despite all Dr. Parker's secrecy, both Professor Curtis and Dr. Harding were probably familiar with the maps Mama had made for Dr. Cope, and knew precisely where we were digging now! And even with that knowledge, they hadn't chosen to excavate in any of Dr. Cope's old sites. Maybe the hadrosaur bone was a fluke. . . .

"I didn't know Mrs. Dancing Moon," I heard Professor Curtis say. "But I know your family was very close to her, Miss Fortune. My sincerest sympathies."

I barely nodded, aware only of a sick feeling in my stomach. Maybe I had led Dr. Parker on a wild-goose chase. And now with Sally gone, I was on my own. Could I find another dinosaur if the excavation at Ghost Horse Canyon played out?

I felt Ned's hand on my arm. Dr. Harding brushed past me, then turned abruptly. "Miss Fortune, I never had the pleasure of meeting your mother, but I understand she was once a capable cartographer and folklorist." She reached for my hand. "Please relay my sympathies on the loss of her old friend."

Dr. Harding was so tiny she had to jump into the stirrup. But she was up in one graceful motion and reined her horse down the hill. Professor Curtis was right behind her. Ned and I watched them disappear in the lengthening Badlands shadows.

"It was thoughtful of her to come," Ned murmured.

"Yes," I admitted, "it was."

Ned turned back toward Sally's hut. "I have to catch a train in Rim tomorrow." He cleared his throat. "Do you want company back to town?"

I shook my head. "I'm headed over to camp."

"We can still ride part of the way together, can't we?"

I nodded, then paused. "Could I change my clothes inside? I'll just be a minute."

Ned unbolted the door and I walked in, carrying Abby's old carpetbag.

It was gloomy and stale inside. Not the place I remembered, where sunshine spilled through the doorway and the bare windows opened to the glittering Badlands. Sally was gone, and so was the spirit, the life she had given these four narrow walls. I pulled out my Tom Fortune clothes and laid them across Sally's cot. I could just make out the brilliant colors of her star quilt. Red. Purple. Orange. The colors of a Badlands sunset. I wondered why the quilt was still here. Surely someone in Ned's family would want it.

I carefully folded my lace shirtwaist and linen skirt into Abby's bag and placed my straw hat on top, hoping it wouldn't get smashed. I'd probably need it again in August when I retired Tom Fortune and assumed my old identity as Tabitha. I glanced around the room one more time, then turned toward the door. How dreary life would be as Tabitha Fortune, school-teacher. I knew now I could never convince Dr. Parker to take me with him back to Yale, not as Tom, and certainly not as Tabitha.

"*One Who Goes Among Ghosts, they have heard you calling.*"

It was Sally's voice. Just like the last time we were together.

I whirled around and stared into the murky gloom of Sally's hut. The room looked back at me unchanged. I jerked on the latch and crossed the threshold quickly. But I felt cold and fluttery, like I used to when Sally told me ghost stories.

"Just a minute." Ned caught the door. "I forgot something."

He crossed to the cot and gathered up Sally's quilt.

"She wanted you to have it," he said, locking the door behind him. "Said you might need it someday."

He had the horses ready, and I looped Abby's carpetbag over the saddle horn. The sky was a soft, buttery color in the west, but sunset was still over an hour away.

"Thank you for the quilt," I said, as we eased down the butte. "I'd like to take it back to camp with me." I glanced down at my carpetbag. "But I don't need this. Would you mind dropping it off with Jesse Hart in town?"

"So Dr. Parker still doesn't know who you really are?"

I reined in Crow. "How did you know?"

"It's pretty obvious." He smiled like Sally.

Then he turned suddenly serious. "You know, Grandmother mentioned you at the end. She told me to remind you of something she said the last time you were together." He paused. "She said to tell you that the ghost horses will come when your heart is clear." He leaned across the saddle and touched my arm. "How can your heart be clear, Tabbie, when you pretend to be someone else?"

For the first time, I felt uncomfortable in my Tom Fortune clothes. Maybe they didn't fit me as well as I thought.

# *Chapter* 27

"We have about two more weeks of work at this site, Thomas," Dr. Parker said. "But I've found no evidence of any more bone. The tibia you found is clearly an isolated fossil. Not uncommon, of course, when working in a primeval setting such as this." He waved his arm toward the canyon wall. "Clearly," he added, turning away, "we need a more productive site."

His words stung. *"An isolated find . . . a more productive site."*

I glanced across the canyon where Dr. Parker's student assistants—Barkley, Doyle, and Adams—were digging and scraping the hadrosaur bone out of sandstone. There had to be more. Perhaps if I could help . . .

I ran to catch up with Dr. Parker, who had crossed the canyon and stood smoking his late-morning cigar with Bill Seymour.

"Excuse me, sir," I asked. "But couldn't I help you here? I'd like to learn your techniques firsthand." Then

I looked straight into Dr. Parker's eyes. "Besides, I believe there's more bone here."

Dr. Parker shook his head. "I disagree, Thomas." He turned away, puffing on his cigar. I knew I'd been dismissed. Then suddenly there were voices high up on the canyon trail—the sound of a woman's laughter.

"Were you expecting anyone, Thomas?" Dr. Parker's eyes narrowed.

"No." I squinted and shaded my eyes. Three riders, one riding sidesaddle.

"Hey, Tom! Tom, you old devil!"

Artie! It was Artie. And Uncle Henry!

I ran toward them both, arms open, then caught myself. Not because I remembered Tom Fortune wouldn't hug his cousin and uncle, but because the woman riding sidesaddle was Janette. Janette Becker. She stopped me in my tracks. Stopped Barkley, Doyle, and Adams, too. They stared at Janette like she was an oasis in the Sahara.

"What *is* the meaning of this, Winslow?" Dr. Parker growled at Uncle Henry. "This is no place for a young lady."

Uncle Henry didn't have time to answer.

"Oh, you must be the *famous* Dr. Parker." Janette smiled, flashing the dimple in her right cheek. "Please don't be angry. I only wanted to meet you and Artie's favorite cousin Thomas. I've heard *sooo* much about you." She bounced out of the saddle and pecked me on the cheek.

It was all I could do not to throw up. But I grinned and tried to look pleased.

"Besides," Janette added, reaching for a hamper secured to her saddle, "I've brought some of Mrs. Porter's famous fried chicken and apple pie for a picnic."

Dr. Parker inspected the hamper, then motioned for Seymour to take it. "All right, young woman. But stay well out of the way—and don't engage in frivolous conversation with my assistants." He glared at Doyle, Adams, and Barkley.

Adams muttered, "Well, if you brought one girl, why couldn't you at least bring one more? You have a sister, don't you, Fortune?"

"Yeah, Fortune." Bill Seymour's eyes narrowed and he flicked his cigar across the top of the hamper. "Where *is* that sister of yours? Haven't seen her around lately."

I cleared my throat and glanced at Uncle Henry for help. His face looked pinched and tight. He was never quick on his feet. Neither was Artie. I realized suddenly that everyone was staring at me. Dr. Parker. Doyle. Adams. Seymour. And Barkley. He was the worst—with a look that seemed to say he knew all about me. I felt sweat beading up under my hat, in my hair—my thick, long black hair bunched up in a braid, hiding there like a coiled snake.

"Oh, you sillies." Janette stomped one beautifully booted foot, soiling its white kid leather. "Didn't you know that Tabitha has joined her parents in Kentucky?

She left last week. Mrs. Winslow is her chaperon. Isn't that lovely?"

She hooked her arm through Bill Seymour's. "Now, tell me, what is *so* fascinating about these beastly old beasts Tom has helped you find."

I glanced at Artie, who smiled back at me. Maybe he was right. Maybe there was more to Janette Becker than I thought.


Uncle Henry and I stood on the far side of the canyon, opposite the excavation. Dr. Parker was eating his third piece of Sister Porter's apple pie. The chicken had been stringy, dry, and tough. As usual. Mama's chicken—and Abby's—was far better.

Uncle Henry explained that he was on a business trip to the School of Mines in Rapid City and had decided to leave a day early to visit me. It had been Artie's idea to come along, too, and to bring Janette.

I watched them together after lunch. She followed him everywhere, as he had followed her the summer before in Mitchell. Together they inspected the excavation, the ramp, the lab tent. She flashed her dimple and tossed her curls and twirled her parasol. But she didn't really flirt with anyone but Artie.

"Have you ever jumped to conclusions about people, Uncle Henry?" I asked, watching Artie and Janette climb the canyon trail. "And then find out just how wrong you were?"

Uncle Henry's blue eyes twinkled. "Then you see it, too?" He took out his pipe, filled it with that spicy-smelling tobacco I'd always loved, then leaned back against the canyon wall. "I wanted something else for Artie this time last year. But I think he knew what he wanted all along. He was right. I was wrong."

"I was wrong about him, too." I paused. "I was wrong about Janette."

Uncle Henry nodded. "You have to let people be who they're meant to be."

I turned away, thinking of Papa. Could Papa ever admit he was wrong about me? That the future he envisioned for me—a good wife and mother married to a man of God—would never make me happy?

"When will you tell Parker who you really are?" Uncle Henry's voice dropped to a whisper.

"He thinks a woman with brains is like a gorilla with two heads."

Uncle Henry chuckled. "At least he and your father have something in common."

"What's so amusing, Thomas?" Dr. Parker asked, wiping his hands across his red-striped vest.

"A family joke," I said quickly, returning to my Tom Fortune voice.

"One of your assistants told me you don't plan to continue digging here," Uncle Henry said. "I believe that's a grave mistake, Phin. The remaining fossils may be hard to reach. You may even need to dynamite. But this site looks extremely promising. I believe there's more bone here."

"This kind of folly must run in the family, Winslow. Your nephew and I were discussing this very issue before your party arrived. I've directed Tom to scout intensively for a more productive site. This is clearly an isolated hadrosaur find."

"Before I'd give up here," Uncle Henry persisted, "I'd put Tom to work digging with your crew."

I wanted to hug Uncle Henry, but Tom Fortune could never do that.

"Impossible. I've paid him to scout, and that's what he'll do." Dr. Parker turned. He squinted at me, then asked, "What makes you so sure there's more bone here, Thomas?"

Dr. Parker seemed to be testing me somehow, measuring my response. I took a deep breath.

"Instinct."

Dr. Parker bent back his head and laughed. A cynical laugh that made me uncomfortable.

"You disappoint me, Thomas," he said, nodding toward Janette, who stood with Artie and Adams across the canyon. "Women rely on instinct. Not scientists. I'll need evidence. *Real* evidence before I'll consider more extensive digging here. Surely you can't argue with that, Winslow."

Dr. Parker squinted at me again, then motioned to his assistants. "Back to work, men!"

I shook hands with Uncle Henry, then with Artie. I even helped Janette climb into the saddle and kissed her hand like a gallant gentleman. "Thank you," I whispered.

"Good luck, Tom," she whispered back. She reached into her pocket and pulled out a letter. I recognized Mama's handwriting at once. "Mrs. Winslow asked that I pass this on to you. She was afraid Mr. Winslow might forget to deliver it."

Then they were off, up the canyon trail winding back to Rim.

# Chapter 28

"A missive of love from the fair Janette?" Doyle's teasing voice spiraled down to me from his position by the hadrosaur tibia on the canyon ledge.

I folded Mama's letter to Aunt Eleanor and slipped it into my vest pocket.

"It looks as though Charles will get his church in Rapid City," she had written.

My eyes felt watery, my cheeks flushed. *Mama.* What would happen to Mama and her work with reservation families? That seemed a lot more important than Papa's "evil age" message to a big church. And what about me? With an entire congregation to impress, now he'd fight my future even harder. I could almost hear his fire-and-brimstone voice: "No God-fearing daughter of mine will study among the demon evolutionists in their ivy-covered towers of sin."

"Heart all aflutter, Fortune?" This time it was Adams.

Tom Fortune wouldn't, couldn't give up. I squared my shoulders. "Jealous, Doyle?" I shouted back.

"That's enough levity, men." Dr. Parker emerged from the lab tent. "You're keeping Thomas from his work." He glanced up at the sky. "There are still four or five hours till dark. We'll see you back at camp for supper, Thomas." Then he turned back inside, where he and Seymour were poring over a fresh supply of scientific journals.

"Nothing on a new carnivorous species, Phin," Seymour murmured.

"Not yet," Dr. Parker replied.

I had just saddled Crow and was reaching for my sample bag when Adams bumped into me. I pitched headfirst into Doyle's knee but managed to hold onto my hat.

"So what's that sister of yours really like, Fortune? Does she wear a hat all the time, too?"

Doyle reached for my hat, but Barkley was quicker. He knocked Doyle off balance, and I ducked around Crow—my hat safely in place, my braid secure underneath.

"We're bald," I fibbed. "That's the gospel truth."

Adams and Doyle laughed. "Must be skinny, too."

My eyes met Barkley's. Why had he intervened?

"Back to work!" Seymour growled from the lab tent.

Doyle and Adams turned back toward the excavation, but Barkley followed me as I led Crow toward the ramp. My stomach felt fluttery, almost sick.

Barkley stopped short. "Listen," he said softly. "I overheard your conversation with Doc Phin this afternoon, and I think you and your uncle are right."

The fluttery feeling stopped, but I felt my heart pounding loud and hard.

"Look," he whispered, his voice earnest and steady. "Everybody heads back to camp around seven for supper. I've volunteered for guard duty these next two weeks. You could meet me back here and we could dig together an hour or so before sunset. Just beyond the hadrosaur trench. Parker says he needs evidence. Let's give him what he wants."

"Why me? Why not Doyle or Adams?"

"You're serious about this. So am I." Barkley paused. "We'd make a good team."

I shook my head. "I don't like working behind Dr. Parker's back."

"It's the only way." Barkley paused again. "Besides," he added slowly, "I'll wager there's a whole side of you that Dr. Parker can't even begin to appreciate."

The fluttery feeling in my stomach came back.

"You've got good instincts," Barkley said, his eyes boring into mine.

I stared back at him for what seemed like hours, then swung into the saddle. "Okay," I said. "I'll be here at seven."

From just after sunup until almost sundown, I spent the next two weeks alone in the Badlands. Just Crow and me and my sample bag. Using Mama's maps, I went places I'd never been before. Rough, isolated canyons; twisted buttes; washed-out gullies. All miles from camp. Miles from the dig. It was tedious, back-breaking work. Leading Crow, I walked over miles and miles of sandstone, straining to see a shard or a fragment of dinosaur bone. But I couldn't find what Dr. Parker was looking for.

"*The ghost horses will come when your mind is clear*."

Sally's voice haunted me. I told myself my mind *was* clear. My conscience was clean. So where were the ghost horses?

Barkley and I weren't successful either. After two weeks of sifting through thin layers of sandstone, we'd found no traces of fossilized bone in the shallow trench beyond the hadrosaur tibia. Maybe Dr. Parker was right and my instincts were wrong. Maybe there weren't anymore dinosaurs in Ghost Horse Canyon.

I rode into camp late that night.

"Ya look like sompum the cat drug in," said Abby, sizing me up. She passed me a cigarette and leaned back against her bedroll.

I held the cigarette between my fingers, watching it burn away. Finally I said, "Maybe I'm cut out to be a schoolteacher after all, Abby." I snuffed out the cigarette.

She shook her head. "I didn't waste my time on no schoolmarm, Tabbie. And my guess is, yer Ma feels the same." She reached into her vest and pulled out a thin, blue envelope. "Jesse delivered it today. Once in a blue moon, he'll do what he should a been doin' all along."

I stared down at the address.

*Miss Tabitha Fortune,*
*c/o Mrs. Abby Hart*
*Rim, South Dakota*

Mama's handwriting was delicate and precise. No one wrote my name more beautifully. I opened the letter slowly.

Dear Tabitha:

I trust Aunt Eleanor has gotten word to you that Papa will get his new church. He is very happy and his sermons have grown even more powerful. I'm reminded of the first summer I knew him, when he was a fiery young evangelist, full of passion. Then, people flocked to the tents where he preached—about making the world a better place for those who had less. He spoke from his heart about his own experiences with poverty. Did you know he was the first person in his family to read and write? So, I married him that summer. Together I believed we could do much good.

But now his message is so different, and I'm reminded of something Sally told me years ago. "He lives by fine words, not by fine deeds." She always saw what others could not see, in your Papa—and in me. Now that she's gone, Tabitha, remember what she said to you. Take her counsel to heart.

All my love,
Mama

I folded the letter away. I would gladly take Sally's counsel to heart, if I only knew what it meant.

It was very late when I crossed the ramp into Ghost Horse Canyon the next night. The shadows were long, but the heat was thick and oppressive, like a crowded church in August. Dr. Parker and Seymour had gone, but Adams and Doyle were still with Barkley. They clustered around a wagon with a massive white-plastered bundle in the back.

"Hey, Fortune," Adams called. "Your dinosaur tibia came down today. Come take a look."

I slid off Crow and walked over to the wagon.

The plastered bone was huge.

"Probably weighs three or four hundred pounds," Adams said, slapping its side. "Could have used another hand getting this thing loaded."

"Sorry I missed it." I started to take off my hat and wipe the sweat beaded on my forehead, but stopped myself in time.

"Should have seen Doc Phin," Doyle joined in. "Looked like a fussy old maid ordering Seymour around."

I smiled and jumped in the wagon seat. The big bulk of plaster that protected the bone filled the wagon box. "Why didn't you take this back to camp today?" I ran my hand across the lumpy plaster surface.

"Doc wants to wait until morning. Feels it's safer then," said Adams.

"Good idea," I said, nodding. "It'll take every mule back at camp to pull this load out." Sweat trickled down my chest. My shirt and vest clung to my body. I tilted my hat and wiped my forehead.

"Say, Fortune," Adams snickered, "I *still* haven't seen you with that hat off."

"I'd wager he sleeps in it," winked Doyle.

"And how do you keep yourself so cool? All buttoned up in that vest."

I was used to their teasing by now, but this time I really didn't look right. All three of them were hatless, their shirts opened to their waists, sleeves rolled up to their elbows.

I jumped out of the wagon and grinned, thinking suddenly of Stephen. "Been swimmin'," I lied. "You know. That stock pond just outside of Rim. You should give it a try."

"Sounds good to me," Adams said, running toward his horse. "Why don't you join us!"

"I'll wait around here a while," I said, turning back to the plastered tibia.

"Too bad you pulled guard duty, Barkley," Adams called out as he crossed the canyon ramp. "See you in the morning!"

I glanced at Barkley. "You're awfully quiet."

He grinned. "Remember when I told you your instincts were good?" Barkley pushed me toward the excavation. "Well, your instincts were right."

He rushed up the ledge and scooped something up from just behind the hadrosaur trench.

My legs suddenly felt like two pillars of lead sunk deep in the canyon floor, and my heart thumped like a cannon on the Fourth of July.

Barkley held out his hand. Three long fossil teeth, each about seven inches long, like the carnivore tooth Dr. Parker had shown me last year in Mitchell. "You were right, Fortune," he repeated. "There's more bone here. Maybe a whole carnivore. But we'll have to blast to get it out."

I threw back my head and laughed, then grabbed my hat and pitched it up to the sky.

My braid thudded against my back. Heavy. Long. Feminine.

I stopped laughing, stopped breathing.

"You won't tell Dr. Parker." My words came out in a rasp.

Barkley, still holding the teeth in his hand, edged closer. "You mean about the teeth?"

"I mean about—"

"This is your story, Fortune. You tell him."

Barkley slipped the teeth in my hand, three curving shafts of long, cool ivory.

"Just don't forget to tell him about the blasting." Barkley winked. "He'll have to order dynamite."

# *Chapter* 29

Dr. Parker and Seymour were waiting for second helpings when I rode into camp. As usual, they sat at their own separate table, complete with real silver and a slightly soiled linen tablecloth. Jesse had forgotten to pick up the camp laundry the day before.

"Mrs. Hart," Dr. Parker called, "more claret!"

Abby stuck her head out of the cook tent and barked back. "Git yer own brew. I'm up to my elbows in venison stew."

Seymour stomped off toward the supply tent.

I swung out of the saddle and looped Crow's reins loosely over the tether line. The carnivore teeth jangled in my vest pocket. My braid was stuffed under my hat. How much should I tell Dr. Parker?

"Good evening, Dr. Parker," I said, standing within the glow of the silver candelabra on his table.

"Fortune." He barely nodded over his crystal goblet as Seymour refilled his glass. "Any luck today?"

"Not exactly what I'd expected."

Dr. Parker's eyes narrowed. "But something promising?"

I reached into my vest pocket and produced the carnivore teeth. I held them under the flickering candlelight. Dr. Parker's eyes widened and he reached for his glasses so quickly that he almost tipped over the claret.

"Where did you find these?" Seymour snarled, taking one of the teeth from my hand.

"Barkley and I found them." I paused. "In Ghost Horse Canyon."

"Impossible!" Seymour held his tooth more closely to the light. "There's nothing left up there."

"Definitely belongs to a Cretaceous carnivore," Dr. Parker said, glancing up at Seymour. "This could be exactly what we've been looking for. Let me see those, Thomas." I dropped them in his hand and he motioned to Doyle and Adams. "Take a look at what your hardworking colleagues have uncovered."

"You know your dinosaur country, Fortune," Adams said. His hair was still damp from his swim.

"Yes, Thomas. Terrific work, though I must say your failure to obey my directives is somewhat shocking, especially for a minister's son, hey?" Dr. Parker laughed at his own joke.

He had never praised me like this before. Only Abby and Uncle Henry's approval had pleased me more. Maybe I had a future in paleontology with Dr. Parker after all.

He backed away from the table. "Where did you say you found these?"

"In a trench just a few feet away from the hadrosaur tibia. Barkley and I have been digging there for the past two weeks."

"Remarkable," Dr. Parker murmured, his voice full of admiration. He turned the teeth over and over in his hands. "Pure instinct. Barkley's always had it—and so do you."

"I thought you said instinct was a female quality, not a scientific one," I said.

Dr. Parker looked up at me coolly. "Some scientists are born with it."

Abby slopped down two bowls of steaming venison stew. She wiped her hands on her skirt. "What kind a critters have those kind a fangs?" she asked, grabbing the dinosaur tooth from Seymour's hand.

Dr. Parker efficiently returned the tooth to Seymour. "You've been hired as a cook, Mrs. Hart, not as a scientist. But if you must know, Barkley and Thomas found these fossilized teeth. Quite significant, actually."

"But what about *instinct*, Dr. Parker?" I persisted. "If it's essentially a female quality, then isn't there a place for women—like Abby and my sister—in the scientific world?"

"You know my views on women in the sciences, Thomas," Dr. Parker grumbled. "Don't disappoint me now."

He set the teeth aside and reached for his soup spoon. He took a long slurp of stew. "Remember, you and Barkley have verified your instincts by supplying evidence. Hard evidence. A feebleminded woman is simply unable to verify her instincts."

Abby spit over Dr. Parker's shoulder, deliberately missing the brass spittoon he'd ordered for her the week before. I reached for one of the teeth and ran my fingers along its edge. Dr. Parker's theory didn't make sense.

"What about A.V. Harding? Surely she's an excellent example of a woman who knows how to verify her instincts."

Dr. Parker's spoon clattered against his bowl. "A two-headed gorilla! Nothing more. If you persist in these ravings, Thomas, I'll ship you back to Rim, regardless of your instincts."

I turned to go, still holding the dinosaur tooth, when I remembered Barkley's last reminder. "Barkley believes my uncle was right," I said. "We'll probably have to blast off the top of the canyon wall to get the rest of the skeleton out."

"That explains why we missed them," Seymour said, setting down his spoon and nodding at the dinosaur teeth.

But Dr. Parker was silent. He reached for his glass of claret, held it up to the light, tipped back his head, and drained the glass. Not a drop escaped. Finally he said, "No doubt, Barkley and Winslow are right." He paused and looked straight at Seymour. "You know what this means, of course?"

Seymour nodded back.

"You and the men ride out in the morning and break up that tibia. I don't want a single shred of evidence that we've found anything—"

"You want to *what?*" I yanked Dr. Parker's arm and claret splashed across the tablecloth. "Break up the tibia? You can't do that!"

"Look what you've done!" Dr. Parker blotted up the beads of red wine.

"You can't destroy that bone. It's priceless."

"It's worthless, kid. Absolutely worthless. It belongs to an established species." Seymour shoved me into Doyle and Adams, then picked up the two teeth lying on the table. "But these . . . Well, *they* could be priceless."

"I've spent the last ten years of my life looking for a find like this, Thomas. I can wait one more year to get it," said Dr. Parker, his eyes glistening. "Surely you understand? I don't want Harding—or anyone else—to rob me of this prize."

He paused, wiping his mouth with the wine-sodden napkin. "Of course, if you can't bring yourself to help us with this endeavor, then I'll write you a check with an ample bonus for the work you've done to date, and ask you to sign a simple nondisclosure agreement, pledging your confidentiality in this matter. You can leave in the morning." Then as an afterthought he added, "I'll make sure that uncle of yours gets a hand-some endowment for his budding new geology department. You see, Thomas, I take care of my friends—even when they don't agree with my methods."

Dr. Parker turned to Doyle and Adams. "Do either of you share Thomas's scruples?"

"Maybe," said Doyle. "But why destroy the tibia? Why not ship it back to Yale like we planned?"

"You picked a bright bunch this time, Phineas." Seymour shook his head and drained his glass. "Ain't any of you smart enough to figure it out?"

Suddenly I understood.

"You'll publicize your failure here," I said, looking beyond Dr. Parker to the stacks of shadowy journals on the table inside his tent. "Then next year, when you have the Badlands all to yourself, you'll come back and blast your carnivore out of the wall. That way you get all the glory. All the credit for finding a new species."

"You're an odd mix of reason and emotion, Thomas." Dr. Parker pushed back from the table. "Still, you're a promising lad, if an overly scrupulous one. Are you with us or against us?"

A wind rustled through the cottonwood overhead, whispering like Sally's ghost horses. I slipped the carnivore tooth I was holding in my vest pocket and looked Dr. Parker straight in the eyes. "I can't let you do this. Call me irrational, emotional, a two-headed gorilla. But I can't let you destroy that tibia." I lifted my hat and my braid tumbled down my back.

"I'll be damned," Seymour whispered.

"Come on, Abby," I said. "Let's get out of here."

I ran toward the horses, hoping Abby was somewhere behind me. I took Crow's reins, then saw that Doyle's gelding was still saddled. I grabbed him for Abby, then slashed the tether line. Suddenly I heard gunshots—probably Seymour firing in the air. Crow and the gelding jumped. The other horses scattered. Where were the mules?

But Abby was behind me, leading all six of them. At that moment, I'd never been so grateful in all my life for Abby's years as a bull whacker. We jumped on the horses and galloped to the trail. In minutes the angry shouts from camp were behind us, and the wagon trace spread out clear and sharp and empty under a full summer moon.

# Chapter 30

We crossed the ramp into Ghost Horse Canyon and I heard a rifle cock.

"It's me," I called out to Barkley. "And Abby Hart."

The canyon glowed silvery white under the moon. Rocks and boulders on the canyon floor were big, black lumps, framing the buckboard and its precious cargo—the hadrosaur tibia. A dark shape wiggled out from behind a wagon wheel.

Barkley held his rifle loosely across his arms. "What's going on?"

"Don't have much time, young feller, so ya better listen up." Abby swung a leg over the saddle and jumped off Doyle's gelding. "Have a smoke. Reckon you'll need it."

Barkley took the cigarette Abby offered. I took one, too. Then I told him about Dr. Parker's plans to smash the plastered bone and come back next summer for the carnivore.

Barkley finished his cigarette without saying a word.

He just stared at the shapeless mound of white plaster in the back of the wagon. Finally he said, "What will you do with it?"

I paused, then said, "I'll take it to Dr. Harding." I glanced at Abby. She nodded her head in agreement. "It's the only way to stop Parker."

Barkley walked around the wagon, running his hand along its side. He stopped just short of me and nodded slowly.

"We'd better get moving," he said at last. "Let me help you with those mules."

They were hitched to the wagon in minutes. Abby climbed in, took the reins, then looked down at me, waiting for my signal to guide the wagon over the ramp. I turned to Barkley.

"Don't worry about keeping my secret," I said. "Dr. Parker knows who I am."

Moonlight spilled across Barkley's face. "Good." He grinned. "Probably a bigger surprise for Doc than the carnivore teeth. Hope you didn't leave them all behind."

I reached for the tooth in my vest and pulled it out, silvery white under the brilliant moon.

"Show it to Harding," he said. "A little hard evidence never hurts."

"Thanks, Barkley." I swung into the saddle, cradling the tooth in my hand. It felt so cool, so light. *Evidence.* Evidence that my instincts about this canyon had been right all along. I glanced up at the north

canyon wall, clear and white and shiny in the moonlight. Sally's voice came to me then, a whisper in the
wind.

*"The ghost horses will come when your heart is clear."*
And that's when I saw it.

First, an empty eye socket. Then the profile of a
skull. There, just a few feet away from the hadrosaur
trench and the carnivore teeth, embedded in the canyon wall, a clear, perfect outline. I couldn't believe we
hadn't noticed it before.

Just at that moment, I heard horses up on the canyon trail. It had to be Seymour and maybe Doyle or
Adams.

"Are you coming with us?" I asked Barkley.

"I'll stay and take care of these guys for you," Barkley
said. He smiled again and slapped Crow on the rump.
My horse leaped ahead. Abby was already moving.

I glanced back at the canyon wall one more time.
No, I hadn't imagined it.

I dug in my spurs and we raced toward the ramp.
The mules balked. Abby swung her whip over their
heads and bellowed. Bullets whizzed by. Seymour was
firing over our heads.

That's all it took.

The wagon lurched forward as the mules pulled it
up the ramp and over the top. It groaned and creaked,
but held. Then the wagon was down the other side.
The precious plaster package hadn't even rolled forward.

Crow's hooves had just hit the trail when I heard the

sound of smashing wood. It must have been Barkley, axing his side of the ramp. I looked over at Abby, who smiled broadly.

"Not ever' day ya meet a man with guts. Let's make tracks."

# Chapter 31

"It's not without precedent," Professor Curtis said. He jumped into the wagon box and examined the white plaster bundle containing the hadrosaur tibia.

The sun was already high overhead, the air dry and hot.

"But it's a throwback to Cope and Marsh. Nobody pulls a stunt like this anymore," Dr. Harding said, brushing a strand of hair away from her face. "Still, we're talking about Phineas. Let me see that tooth again, Tabitha."

I handed it to Dr. Harding and she ran her fingers along its indentations. "It could belong to a new species. What do you think, Charlie?" She passed the tooth to Professor Curtis.

"Very likely. I've never seen anything quite like it."

"And you're sure, Tabitha, about the skull?" Dr. Harding's voice was steady and sure.

"Yes. I know I saw it." My voice was just as steady, just as sure. If I closed my eyes, I knew I'd see it again.

A clear, sharp outline against the silver canyon wall.

"Then it's time to pay a professional call on the illustrious Dr. Parker." Dr. Harding started for the horses tethered at the edge of the plateau, then turned back to Abby and me. "Charlie and I are a little short-handed these days. Tabitha, my original offer still holds. Parker's salary plus an extra two dollars a week. That goes for you, too, Mrs. Hart. Will you join us?"

I didn't mean to hesitate, but a lump rose in my throat. For a second or two, I wasn't sure I could even talk. This job was real, for me. For Tabitha. I shook Dr. Harding's hand and mumbled, "Sure."

Abby wiped her hands on her skirt. "You betcha. Shoulda started here in the first place, Tabbie. Always work fer folks who know how ta appreciate ya."

At that moment, a band of riders crested the plateau. Seymour, Doyle, and Adams. Dr. Parker brought up the rear, perspiration beading on his forehead. He sat straight in the saddle. Seymour's hand rested on the stock of his rifle.

"We've come for that tibia, Harding." Dr. Parker's voice boomed out like Papa's. "And if you resist, I'll sue you and Princeton for every dime in your second-rate institution." He took out a white linen handkerchief and wiped his forehead. "Professional espionage with amateurs like these." He gestured toward Abby and me. "How you've lowered yourself, Annabelle Harding."

I exchanged a look with Abby. So he thought we

were spies! Yet he'd had me spy on Dr. Harding and Professor Curtis almost from the beginning. I moved quietly around the edge of the wagon and slowly reached for the double-barreled shotgun under the wagon seat. I slid in behind the professor, out of Seymour and Dr. Parker's view.

"That bone stays right here." Dr. Harding's eyes narrowed.

Seymour patted his rifle stock. "We outnumber you. Four *men* to one." He started to pull out his rifle.

But I was quicker. I cocked the shotgun and aimed right between Seymour's eyes. "Drop the rifle, Seymour. That bone stays here."

He snorted, still reaching for his gun.

"She's a dead shot, Seymour. And so am I." Abby leveled her six-shooter at Seymour. "Throw down that rifle and clear outta here."

He pitched his rifle toward the wagon. Professor Curtis scooped it up. "What about the rest of you. Any guns?"

"Nothin' to worry 'bout," Abby spit again. "Just a passel a sissies. Not a one but Seymour could hit the broad side of a barn."

Seymour winced at the word *sissies*, but what Abby said was true.

Dr. Harding turned to face Dr. Parker. She jerked on his horse's bridle, pulling Parker close. "Just count yourself lucky that I won't report this to the American Academy of Science. But if you take me to court, I'll expose you to every scientist in North America. Pack up your bags and get out of here."

Sweat rolled down Dr. Parker's forehead and neck, collecting around his high, tightly starched collar, spreading across his striped vest.

"Well, perhaps I've been hasty, Annabelle," Dr. Parker said smoothly. "There's obviously been a misunderstanding all around." He dabbed his forehead again. "The girl there got me muddled. Just let us take our mules and the tibia and we'll forget all about this."

"You can have your mules. But the bone stays here," Dr. Harding said. She motioned for Abby to get the mules. "I can't entrust precious dinosaur cargo to a man who would smash Cretaceous bones to further his own career." She turned and walked toward her lab tent.

"Let's bury the hatchet, A.V. Work Ghost Horse Canyon together," Dr. Parker called out.

Dr. Harding disappeared inside the tent.

"You have no right to dig there," Parker shouted. "Fortune's been working for me since September. That's *my* carnivore up there. My team found it first."

"*You* have no right to dig in Ghost Horse Canyon," I bristled back, suddenly remembering Mama's maps. "Dr. Cope found Ghost Horse Canyon first—seven years ago—and Dr. Harding was part of his *original* team. She has every right to go back there and dig."

Professor Curtis threw back his head and laughed.

"You don't have a leg to stand on, Parker. You're finished here."

Dr. Parker scowled down at me. "I'll teach you a lesson you'll never forget, young lady. Science has no place for two-faced creatures like you." He turned his horse and galloped off the plateau. Seymour and Adams followed with the mules. Doyle stayed behind.

"Don't worry about Phin. He's full of hot air." He grinned. "Good luck, Fortune."

We shook hands.

"What happened to Barkley?" I asked.

"Parker fired him. But he has a standing offer to work with Henry Osborn at the Geological Survey. Barkley's a natural—like you. He'll come out all right." Doyle tipped his hat at Abby. Then he was gone.

I walked to the edge of the plateau and watched the riders until they disappeared like a mirage in the Badlands haze. I hoped I'd never see or hear from Dr. Parker again. And I tried not to think about his threat.


The next day we drove the hadrosaur tibia into Rim. Abby had volunteered to put it under lock and key in her back room at the post office. After we hoisted our plaster bundle in through the wide double doors out back, it filled the whole space inside. Jesse wasn't too happy about it because it meant he couldn't squeeze into the back room to sort mail.

"Don't matter none," Abby cackled. "Jesse's so dad-burned slow anyway, nobody'll know the differnz."

But he handed me two letters.

One was from Mama, saying they would be home sooner than expected. The other was from Barkley. A big envelope. Thick and bumpy. Inside there was no letter—just the two carnivore teeth I'd left behind in Dr. Parker's camp.

# Chapter 32

We rode to Ghost Horse Canyon at dawn the next day. I led Dr. Harding and Professor Curtis through Dr. Parker's old camp, then across the narrow, zigzag trail that descended into the canyon from the west. The north wall where I'd seen the carnivore's skull was still in deep shadow when we reached the canyon floor.

I looked up at the wall, just west of the hadrosaur ledge.

The skull wasn't there.

Or at least, I couldn't see it. Neither did Dr. Harding or Professor Curtis.

"You're sure you didn't imagine it," he said slowly.

"I'm *sure*." I'd never been so sure of anything in my life.

I crossed to the opposite side of the canyon, toward the busted-up ramp. Young, tender rays of morning light filtered over the east wall, spilling into the canyon.

I turned and called back to Professor Curtis, "Let's wait a few more minutes."

The light was soft, silvery. The shadows on the

north wall lightened, like the sky under a full moon. Slow, pale, and subtle. I waited. So did Dr. Harding and Professor Curtis. We waited for the light to cross the entire wall.

And then, suddenly, there it was.

First an eye, then the jaw, then the whole profile.

"Look!" I said softly, pointing up at the carnivore. I felt as light and airy as the sky overhead, as if I'd jumped off Ghost Horse Canyon and flown across it.

Professor Curtis shot me a smile.

Dr. Harding nodded. "Very impressive."

We moved closer to the canyon wall. Dr. Harding tilted her hat back and squinted up at the carnivore's profile.

"Your uncle was right about one thing, Tabitha," she said. "This animal is deeply embedded in its matrix. But blasting could be tricky."

Professor Curtis frowned. "We could lose one whole side of the skull and risk losing more teeth if we dynamite." He took off his hat and wiped his forehead. "But I don't see how we can get to the skeleton any other way."

Destroy half the skeleton to preserve the other half? No, there had to be an alternative.

I stepped back and looked up at the sheer sandstone wall. The skull was about twenty feet above us, maybe six feet from the ledge where Barkley and I had found its teeth, a good fifteen feet from the canyon's crest. I ran my hand over the sandstone wall. We could carve footholds in the rock and climb up. But the wall here was smooth and slick. Once we reached the skull, how could we keep our balance as we dug? The only indentation in the rock—a low, shallow slit—was above the skull, and that clearly wouldn't help. No, an approach from the canyon floor would be impossible.

But what about from the top down? Could we scale down the top of the canyon wall, remove the skull and the rock surrounding it, then haul it all back over the crest?

"I may have an idea," I said slowly.

We spent the next three days moving Dr. Harding's supplies to Ghost Horse Canyon, hauling water in from Parker's old camp, and rebuilding the ramp. If all went well, the carnivore's skull, the hadrosaur tibia, and Professor Curtis's *Triceratops* would be on their way back to Princeton by mid-July.

A full week before I expected Papa.

# *Chapter* 33

First Professor Curtis and then Dr. Harding went down over the top of the canyon. It had rained the night before, and the sandstone was slippery. But both were as surefooted as Abby's mules. From where I stood, I could see Dr. Harding wielding her pick several feet below the carnivore's jaw. Professor Curtis was to her left, also carving out a foothold. A chunk of sandstone broke free. It skittered down the wall and smashed on the canyon floor.

Two hours later, Abby and I hauled them up. Dr. Harding's arms were shaking. Professor Curtis had leg cramps. But beneath the skull, they had created a narrow ledge, just wide enough for two people to stand on.

"Let me spell one of you," I pleaded, refilling Dr. Harding's canteen.

She drank slowly, then shook her head. "Too dangerous."

Professor Curtis walked stiffly down the grassy ledge toward the trail and back. He motioned to Dr. Harding. "Let's keep working while it's cool." He filled his canteen and stuck a few strips of jerky in his pocket. "Take it easy going over that ledge down there," he said, pointing to the narrow slit in the sandstone a few feet above the skull. "A little rough last time."

Dr. Harding tightened the rope around her waist, and we both watched as Abby fed Professor Curtis the rope.

I saw the rattler before I heard it. It flashed out at the professor from the ledge, struck him just below the knee. It dangled there like a funnel cloud, fangs caught on his heavy trousers. Instinctively, I pulled out my revolver and shot. Once. Twice. The snake jerked and fell to the ground.

Abby and Dr. Harding guided Professor Curtis back over the top. His face was drained of color.

"Good shot," he whispered.

Abby knelt and slit the professor's pant leg open. There were two faint marks, tiny pinpoints surrounded by a mound of bluish flesh.

"Damn," Dr. Harding muttered. She pulled off her vest and stuffed it under his head.

Remembering what I'd learned from Mama, I tied my bandanna tight around his leg just above the snakebite, then ran for the canteen of whiskey I knew Abby kept behind the wagon seat. I handed Professor Curtis the canteen and he took two long gulps. He passed it up to Abby as she pulled out her old bowie knife from Deadwood days.

"I think I'm going to faint," he laughed weakly.

"Nothin' to be ashamed of under the circumstances. I've done it a few times myself." She smiled grimly, shoving Dr. Harding and me out of the way. "Give me some room here, ladies."

I'd never seen Abby work so fast. She doused whiskey over the knife, made a short clean incision lengthwise over the bite, then leaned over to suck the venom out of the wound. She spit the last of the poison over the side of the canyon, wiped her mouth, and gargled with what remained of the whiskey. She spit that out, too.

"Don't think the bite's too bad," she said at last. "But ya niver know. We gotta git him to a real doctor."

"I'll drive him into Rim." Dr. Harding was already moving toward the mules.

"But do you know the country well enough?" The question was out of my mouth before I had time to think.

Dr. Harding almost grinned. "I've been here before, remember? Besides," she added grimly, "if anything happens to Charlie, I'll need to wire his wife."

We hitched up the team in silence. Abby and Dr. Harding carried Professor Curtis to the wagon. I ran down to camp for blankets and water, and snatched Sally's quilt from my tent. Maybe that would bring him good luck. I climbed into the wagon and tucked the quilt around Charlie's body. He was already beginning to shiver. His face was so pale, so white. He didn't look like a robust dinosaur hunter anymore.

Abby joined me down at camp and we watched as Dr. Harding took the wagon over the ramp and turned west along the old wagon trace toward Rim. It would take her at least three hours to get there.

"I've seen worse," Abby rasped. "But he's tough. He'll make it, Tabbie."

I turned and looked up at the carnivore's skull. The noonday sun was so blinding, I could just barely make out its profile. I thought of the long afternoon stretching out ahead of us. Sitting idle would be unbearable.

"Come on, Abby. We have work to do—for the professor."

I knotted Dr. Harding's rope around my waist and looked over at Abby.

"Take me down easy," I said.

Abby took out a chew—a big one. She rolled it around her mouth and squinted at me. Finally she said, "Be kearful, Tabbie. Remember, snakes come in pairs." She secured Dr. Harding's line around a hefty sandstone boulder, then wound up the slack around her elbow.

I tucked my pick under my left arm and slung my collecting bag with all my hand tools across my right shoulder. Then I was over the edge, just inches above the narrow slit where the rattler had been. I tightened my grip on the pick under my arm, readjusted my weight, then dropped my right hand to my holster. My left arm tensed, but my hold felt tight, secure. I pulled out my Smith & Wesson and looked down at the ledge. It was so narrow, almost hidden by a slight overhang. I held my breath, listening for a rattle. I heard nothing but my pounding heart.

First my feet, then my legs slid past the opening. Still no sound from the ledge.

My arms and chest inched past. Then my chin. My mouth felt so dry.

I closed my eyes, deciding it would be worse to see a rattler strike me on the nose than to feel it. When I opened my eyes again, the ledge was four feet above me. My feet brushed against the narrow ledge Dr. Harding and Professor Curtis had carved in the morning, and the rope went slack. I let out my breath and slipped my six-shooter back in its holster.

I was face to face with the dinosaur. My hand traced where its eye had once been. Had its eyes been yellow or green? Brown? Purple? Orange? What would it think of me? A snack between lunch and supper? I laughed and Abby called down, "Anything wrong?"

"No! I'm fine. Just fine." Never better.

I reached into my bag and pulled out an awl. I traced the line a few inches above the dinosaur's skull where Dr. Harding had been working in the morning. That's where I began. Chipping away at the matrix, following a pink sandstone line that arched over the skull.

I worked in quarter inches. Slowly. Very slowly. Heat radiated off the canyon wall, and sweat trickled down my face, neck, chest. But I barely noticed it. The world long past was much more compelling than the present. I looked into what had been the dinosaur's eye and wondered how it had cared for its young. Did it lay eggs like prairie rattlers in a den? I shivered, suddenly thinking of Professor Curtis. I opened my canteen and drank a few sips of tepid water.

I don't know how long I worked in Ghost Horse Canyon that afternoon. But it didn't seem long before Abby's voice rang out.

"We've got company."

# Chapter 34

It was Papa. Tall and dark and stern in a brand-new suit. His face reminded me of a picture I'd seen once of Moses when he found the children of Israel dancing around the Golden Calf.

"What have you done?" His voice bellowed across the canyon. If he'd had a set of stone tablets he would have smashed them at my feet.

Abby inched closer, but I motioned her away. "Leave us alone awhile, Abby."

She nodded. Her spurs jingled as she walked heavily down the trail.

I turned my back on Papa and slid the collecting bag off my shoulder. "How did you know where to find me?" I asked, propping my pick against a boulder.

"A Dr. Phineas Parker," he said, pronouncing each word slowly, dramatically. "Does the name mean nothing to you?"

"I worked for him this summer," I said softly.

"Liar!" Papa spit out the word and hurled it at me. "*Liar!* You spied on him. Assumed a false identity.

Became a *man*. 'Be not deceived: neither idolaters, nor thieves, nor drunkards, nor revilers, nor extortioners, shall inherit the kingdom of God.' "

"But I'm not any of those things." I turned to face Papa. When would he learn to see me as I really was? I reached into my pocket, where I still carried Barkley's dinosaur teeth. "I just want to know about the world *before* we got here. What the world was like before Adam and Eve."

" 'And the earth was without form, and void,' " Papa quoted.

"No, Papa." I held out one of the teeth. "This animal was here before we were. You can't argue with this kind of evidence."

He picked up the tooth and held it high in his hand. For a moment, I thought he was going to pitch it over the canyon, smash it into a million pieces. But he lowered his arm and turned the tooth over in his hands.

"The Devil's instrument." Papa's hand shook. "This is the work of the Devil."

"You're wrong. It belonged to an animal that died here, *here*, millions of years ago."

Papa looked up at me. His eyes were wild. "The work of the Devil, I say!" he called out, and the Badlands rang with his shout. "Come away with me, Tabitha Ruth! Now. Before it's too late! 'Come out from among them, and be ye separate, saith the Lord, and touch not the unclean thing.' "

"I'm not coming with you," I said. "This is where I belong."

The light went out of his eyes, but his hands still shook. He dropped the tooth, "the unclean thing," into my open hands.

" 'Depart from me,' " he said softly, " 'ye that work iniquity. . . .' "

I stared into his eyes for just an instant. They didn't flicker. I'd been dismissed, banished. But I had finally won my freedom. Papa had given in, given up.

As he turned to go, his shoulders stooped in his well-cut suit, I realized then that—despite the church in Rapid City, the crowds he would draw, the praises he'd receive—from this day forward, Papa would consider himself a failure. Because he had failed to bring his own daughter into his fold.

He walked to his horse and swung slowly into the saddle.

And then, suddenly, there was Mama. Hatless, her hair tussled, her face flushed. She slid off Ransom and looked first at me, then at Papa.

"We've lost her, Dorothy," Papa said, his voice raspy. "Satan has claimed her, heart and soul."

Mama glanced back at me and smiled. "You've really found your calling then?"

I nodded.

Mama looked up at Papa, her eyes misty, her voice soft. "I'm not going with you either, Charles. I don't know what I'll do. But I'm not going with you."

Papa's jaw dropped, but his voice grew hard. "How will you live, Wife?"

"The way I should have always lived. Following my

heart." Mama walked to my side. "Tabitha's taught me that. I'm alive again, Charles, and I can't go back."

Papa stared out over the canyon, then turned his horse down the trail. He looked small somehow. Insignificant. I slipped my arm around Mama's waist. We watched him go together. Out of sight and into the distant Badlands.

Above us, the Dakota sky arched so blue, so wide, so vast. The song of a western meadowlark floated across the canyon like the calling of Sally's ghost horses. I watched the bird winging toward the horizon, toward a destination I couldn't see. And for some reason, it reminded me of a dinosaur.

# DON'T MISS ANY OF THE STORIES
# BY AWARD-WINNING AUTHOR
# AVI

AVAILABLE IN BOOKSTORES EVERYWHERE
OR SEE BELOW FOR ORDERING INFORMATION

☐ THE BARN                          72562-2/$4.99 US/$6.99 Can

☐ BLUE HERON                        72043-4/$4.50 US/$6.50 Can

☐ THE MAN WHO WAS POE               71192-3/$4.99 US/$6.99 Can

☐ NOTHING BUT THE TRUTH             71907-X/$4.99 US/$6.99 Can

☐ A PLACE CALLED UGLY               72423-5/$4.50 US/$5.99 Can

☐ POPPY                             72769-2/$4.99 US/$6.99 Can

☐ PUNCH WITH JUDY                   72253-4/$4.50 US/$5.99 Can

☐ ROMEO AND JULIET TOGETHER
   (AND ALIVE!) AT LAST            70525-7/$4.50 US/$5.99 Can

☐ SOMETHING UPSTAIRS                70853-1/$4.50 US/$6.50 Can

☐ SOMETIMES I THINK I HEAR
   MY NAME                         72424-3/$4.50 US/$5.99 Can

☐ S.O.R. LOSERS                     69993-1/$4.50 US/$5.99 Can

☐ THE TRUE CONFESSIONS OF
   CHARLOTTE DOYLE                 71475-2/$4.99 US/$6.99 Can

☐ "WHO WAS THAT MASKED
   MAN, ANYWAY?"                   72113-9/$3.99 US/$4.99 Can

☐ WINDCATCHER                       71805-7/$4.99 US/$6.99 Can